Surviving in Sea Breezes

By

Douglas Thornblom

Copyright © June, 2017 by Douglas Thornblom

All rights reserved. No part of this publication may be reproduced, distributed, or transmitted in any from or by any means, including photocopying, recording, or other electronic or mechanical methods, without the prior written permission of the author.

This is a work of fiction. Names, characters, businesses, places, events and incidents are either the products of the author's imagination or used in a fictitious manner. Any resemblance to actual persons, living or dead, or actual events is purely coincidental.

Cover photo courtesy of Pixabay

Other Books by Douglas Thornblom

Defending Sea Breezes

The English Winemaker, a novella

DEDICATION

This book is dedicated to all the men and women in America who have ever worn a uniform and put themselves into harm's way in defense of their communities and their nation. No one who hasn't been in your shoes and boots could possibly appreciate all that you have risked, and all that you have done, for your fellow Americans. God bless you all.

My late friend, West Point classmate, and fellow Army Ranger, LTC (RET) Michael E. Oshel, is one of these men- a true warrior, and one of the toughest guys I've ever known. Well done, Mike.

"We sleep safely at night because rough men stand ready to visit violence on those who would harm us."

Attributed to George Orwell

"No arsenal, or no weapon in the arsenals of the world, is as formidable as the will and moral courage of free men and women."

Ronald Reagan

Table of Contents

PROLOGUE
CHAPTER 1
CHAPTER 2
CHAPTER 3
CHAPTER 4
CHAPTER 5
CHAPTER 6
CHAPTER 7
CHAPTER 8
CHAPTER 9
CHAPTER 10
CHAPTER 11
CHAPTER 12
CHAPTER 13
CHAPTER 14
CHAPTER 15
CHAPTER 16
CHAPTER 17
CHAPTER 18
CHAPTER 19
CHAPTER 20
CHAPTER 21
CHAPTER 22
CHAPTER 23
CHAPTER 24
CHAPTER 25
CHAPTER 26
CHAPTER 27

CHAPTER 28
CHAPTER 29
CHAPTER 30
CHAPTER 31
CHAPTER 32
CHAPTER 33
CHAPTER 34
CHAPTER 35
CHAPTER 36
CHAPTER 37
CHAPTER 38
CHAPTER 39
CHAPTER 40
CHAPTER 41
CHAPTER 42
CHAPTER 43
CHAPTER 44
CHAPTER 45
CHAPTER 46
CHAPTER 47
CHAPTER 48
CHAPTER 49
CHAPTER 50
CHAPTER 51
CHAPTER 52
CHAPTER 53
CHAPTER 54
EPILOGUE

EPILOGUE FROM DEFENDING SEA BREEZES

3-4 June

It was Sean Koenig who first saw the helicopter, a Florida National Guard Blackhawk, flying over the Port Monroe oil refinery and downtown area from his rooftop guard position. He was so excited he fired off three rounds from his rifle out towards the ocean. This of course brought a reaction from the Quick Reaction Force (QRF) team on duty as well as alarming the whole neighborhood, which in hindsight, was as good a way as any to get the word out. Certainly no one was angry with the young man for alerting everyone to the good news.

In the United States, the president had continued the periodic updates, and the FEMA national emergency radio system had been restored in the first week in March. Even so, the president had used both the FEMA radio system and the Ham radio network to send out his communications, since most citizens were used to getting the messages on their battery-powered Ham radios, and the power was still out over the majority of the country.

Although the messages always had an encouraging outlook, reading between the lines it was obvious that the government was still struggling with the problem of trying to settle the millions who had fled the dirty bomb target areas, as well as the millions who had fled all the other large cities and military bases fearing similar attacks.

The situation had been comparatively peaceful and uneventful in Sea Breezes over the last two months. There were no major security events, except for two night attacks by small groups- apparently unsuspecting elements from Port Monroe- who were unaware of Sea Breezes' defenses. The attacks were quickly repelled by the roof guards, assisted by quick-reacting homeowners in the areas hit. By the time the QRF teams on duty had arrived, the attackers had already been driven off, and there were no casualties among the Sea Breezes' fighters.

A sort of non-aggression pact had been made with the Zulu Warriors in Pelican's Landing when Richard had led a contingent of two QRF teams out to Sunset Beach Estates for a talk, similar to what they had done in the prisoner exchange with the Werewolves. After an initial verbal standoff, Richard had met with the gang's leader at the gated entrance. After a brief discussion they agreed it was in their best interests to leave each other alone, since they all knew that the government was in the initial phases of reconstituting, and help would probably be arriving to Port Monroe soon.

Richard reminded the gang leader that sooner or later the military or law enforcement authorities would take a dim view of the Zulus having killed scores of people and stolen their houses, and that they might want to think about moving back to Port Monroe to their own turf soon. They hadn't yet, but Richard knew they wouldn't be in Pelican's Landing when the Army or police forces arrived, especially now that the first Army helicopter had been seen over the city.

By the beginning of June, the situation in Sea Breezes had stabilized, as the community adjusted to the "new normal" of their harsh existence. More frequent scavenging trips, targeting every possible source of food and supplies, including abandoned homes as well as small stores of all types, had yielded not only some food, but also some medical supplies. The improved security situation allowed them to take more time to thoroughly search more areas in detail. Locked storage rooms and cabinets in the upper floors of the hospital, and in the island's CVS and Walgreens stand-alone pharmacies, yielded some more antibiotics, prescription drugs, and over the counter medicine and other medical supplies. Julia was very pleased, because her aid station was better able to handle most of the community's medical problems.

Sea Breezes had sustained a few more deaths: two more men had died of complications from gunshot wounds sustained during the previous Werewolves' attack; one woman had died in childbirth from loss of blood; and there had been one fatal heart attack and one suicide. But otherwise her patient load was down, and consisted mostly of non-life-threatening illnesses and diseases, such as flu, diarrhea, infections, skin rashes, and sprains.

Canned and packaged food had been found in a few of the stores, homes, and restaurants they had searched, and the first vegetables from their home and community gardens were being harvested. There were even some oranges and grapefruit popping up at the weekly Sea Breezes "bazaars" from back yard trees neighbors had planted when they first moved into the Sea Breezes. Richard and Sophia had delighted over their first tomato and first orange in three months, and they had gotten used to eating a lot of fish. They, like everyone else, had lost considerable weight, and some of their less prepared neighbors were downright thin.

Fish had become more plentiful because the fishermen had been able to branch out to other areas, accompanied by their security forces, and now went out every other day and stayed out fishing longer. The hunters still brought in some varied types of meat, but the supply of edible animals was almost exhausted on the small island. Fortunately, with winter ending in Canada, flocks of geese often paused from their journey northward to rest in their lake, and many were harvested. But the lake's duck population had long since been depleted.

The Koenigs and the Cantrells had only a few items left of packaged food left to eat- actually just a few large containers of freeze dried meals and a few MREs. Both families had given away some of their supplies to families in need who had children to feed.

After the second sighting of helicopters, this time of several scout helicopters over both the city and the Port Monroe airport, the old friends met at the Koenigs' house to celebrate, and after a meager dinner, the four adults sat down with the last of their Jack Daniels and Cokes. Their shared evening meal had consisted of some fish, a freeze-dried mix of berries, a few MRE crackers, and two small tomatoes.

Anita and Sean were in the front yard playing with Natasha, who wasn't quite as lively as she was before her wound. She was still fairly young so she healed quickly, although not completely. Like Richard, she would always have a bit of a limp. But she was again able to enjoy being chased, and fetching tennis balls for the kids. Natasha had also lost a lot of weight, but after saving Richard's life, there was no way that he was not going to feed her regularly. Not all of the families in the neighborhood did that for their pets.

Sophia took her first sip in months of their favorite Jack and Coke drink, smiled and sighed. "I'm glad we saved a little for this occasion. I'm getting really tired of drinking only water that has a Clorox taste. Who knows when we'll get a chance to have real drinks again?"

Carmen smiled and said, "Yeah, I guess it'll be a while, but what I miss the most is being able to take a long, hot shower. Bathing out of a bucket is not my idea of clean. I think that's what I'm most looking forward to in the future. It's funny how the little things we've always taken for granted are what we miss the most."

Richard said, "Well it goes without saying that we all miss having a steady supply of all kinds of food whenever we wanted it. Just think about how great it would be now to be able to drive down and get a Big Mac for supper."

There was a contemplative silence over these thoughts, until the quiet was broken by Josh. "Rich, did you ever think we'd be fighting battles again? Man, I retired to get away from being shot at, but as soon as I got to my retirement home, I had to go to war again."

Richard looked at his old friend and said, "Yeah, but I think we did pretty good, helping to organize a group of civilians to defend themselves. Many of the men and women worked as hard as we did, and some were truly heroic; I'm thinking of people like Donna, Jacob, Bill and Julia. And, let's face it; it takes a lot of dedication and bravery to be a rooftop guard. Everyone was at the very least cooperative- even Fred Carlucci- once he realized that we were on our own. It just goes to show you that Americans can still rise to the occasion and take up arms to defend themselves and their communities when they have to."

"Yeah" Josh said, "and I won't forget the other veterans, especially Leroy Ivory- that man makes me proud to be a Marine. All of the vets pitched in with help and encouragement wherever they could. But man, I'm just glad it's coming to an end soon. We still have a ways to go though. It ain't over 'til it's over."

At the end of the evening, as the sun was setting over the horizon of the Sea Breezes homes, Sophia and Richard, with Natasha at their side, strolled back to their house, hand in hand. When they got home, Richard and Sophia undressed, gave each other a long kiss, and went to bed, snuggled in each other's arms.

The next morning, after Sophia and Richard had finished their small breakfast and fed Natasha, they heard a loud and unfamiliar sound above them. They ran out into the front yard to see what the racket was. They saw an amazing sight- three Air Force C-130 cargo planes had flown near Phelps Island and were descending slowly on short final approach to the Port Monroe airport.

Richard and Sophia were overjoyed at the sight- help was on its way soon. They hugged each other and pointed up to the sky, as other neighbors came out to see what was going on. Everyone was shouting and jumping for joy, and Natasha, sensing their strange behavior as happiness, started barking and dancing around them. Richard picked Sophia up and swung her around as they both laughed and cried at the same time. He put her down, put his hands on her face, and said, "We did it, honey. We're gonna make it. I love you very much."

He kissed her, wrapped his arm around her slender waist, and walked her up their sidewalk and into their home, Natasha leading the way. As he crossed the threshold, a sobering thought crossed Richard's mind. This wasn't just the end; it was also a new and uncertain beginning.

Chapter 1

5 June

Richard Cantrell woke up to the dawn light streaming through the bedroom window, after a long night of tossing and turning. He sat up, rubbed his eyes, and sighed. He looked over at the empty space next to him and remembered that Sophia was still on her shift of rooftop guard duty, so he lay back down in bed for a few more minutes, his mind going over some of the previous evening's thoughts.

His initial relief and joy at seeing the C-130's land at Port Monroe's airport the day before had given way last night to pondering how things would play out in the future for the community of Sea Breezes. So far they had neither seen nor heard anything from the force that had landed, whoever they were. What was the force here for?

Rich was an experienced Infantryman and Army Ranger- a retired Lieutenant Colonel with four years of combat in the Middle East, and the battle scars to prove it. He was awake most of the night analyzing the implications of what this small landing force that had just arrived the day before could mean.

Rich calculated that the C-130's most likely landed about a company of Infantry, along with their equipment and supplies, and probably some logistics experts on port and refinery operations. With all that had happened to the armed forces the past four months, and the long list of missions the Army must have on its plate, the force could be as few as 100 soldiers, about half the size of a normal company. And, those troops would likely be a mixture of forces from several peacetime companies, and possibly even a composite company made up of National Guard, Reserve, and Regular Army soldiers, what with the attacks on several Army posts, and the disruption of the Reserves and National Guard soldiers due to family considerations after the Collapse. At any rate, they were sure to have brought along a couple of Humvees, and enough food, ammo, and fuel to last... how long?

He didn't really know, and that's what bothered him. Their mission could be just a quick recon-in-force to assess the status of the city, port, and oil refinery- in and out in a week or less. Or, they could be the advance party of a larger follow-on force intent on occupying and rebuilding. There were just so many questions, possibilities, and unknowns out there. It was that realization, and the resulting very different consequences for Sea Breezes, that had kept him awake for most of the night.

Whatever the force's mission was, he knew what their immediate priorities would be to clear and secure the runway and then the airport buildings. Once they accomplished that, they would set up a perimeter defense, offload supplies, and establish a headquarters in one of the buildings. That could be easy, or it could be difficult if one of the city gangs had taken up residence in the airport buildings and hangers.

He also knew that even if they hadn't, some gang might try to probe the defenses of the newly arrived troops and try to capture some of the ammunition and food they had brought with them. He hoped the company commander was experienced enough to quickly find a secure and protected storage facility for his supplies, and to put a heavy 24/7 guard on them.

Rich also realized that even if there were a follow-on force in the works, reaching out to the various communities in and around Port Monroe would not be among the force's objectives. After securing the airport, their first mission would be to secure and control the strategically important parts of the city, such as the port docks and facilities, and the oil refinery. These would certainly have to be among the main types of infrastructure that the president and his staff would be trying to get operational along America's coastal cities. The president had to put the devastated country back together again, and that meant getting the elements of the economy operating, including trade and fuel supplies. Port Monroe probably barely made the cut to be important enough to consider a recon-in-force.

If there were a follow-on force planned after the initial forces secured the airport, port, and oil refinery, more troops would be brought in to recon the city to see how bad things were and to find out if there was any semblance of a city government left that they could put together. They would also have to secure the roadways to and from the port and the refinery, and then evaluate the extent of damage, and how much and what type of work and equipment would be needed to get them operational again- not an easy task, especially since the refinery had suffered explosions and burning from terrorist attacks. They must know something about the extent of the damage by aerial surveillance though.

And the city gangs would certainly not go away easily. MS-13 had a large presence in the city before the Collapse, and they were the most ruthless and unpredictable of the lot. Any surviving gang members, of any flavor, would surely protect their new turf, knowing that surrender would mean jail at best, and in these times, more likely a firing squad. If they were smart, they would leave the small force alone to wait and see if they left or not.

At any rate, all of that meant that Sea Breezes wasn't going to be rescued any time soon, and he realized that he would have to make that clear at today's community meeting at the lake. He also knew it would be a depressing dose of reality that would not be welcomed by his neighbors, who had already endured four months of hardship and deprivation.

Right after the Collapse, Rich and his brother-in-law, Josh Koenig, had more or less been chosen (actually, they had volunteered) to make up a security plan for Sea Breezes, and to lead the foraging operations to find food, medical supplies, tools, and other necessary items. The scavenging parties had been successful so far, that is, after having been ambushed when they had gone out on their first scavenging mission. The few guards he had left behind to secure the vehicles had been viciously attacked by redneck thugs in pickup trucks while most of the men and women he had taken along were scavenging in a store. The guards had been attacked in an assault by redneck thugs in pickup trucks. He had lost some of his neighbors in that attack, before he and the other team members could react, and from then on he had taken more vehicle guards with him.

So, his task this morning was to be the bearer of bad news, and he didn't relish the talk he had to give to his neighbors. Rich got dressed and went out to the back porch to light a small fire in the BBQ grill so he could warm up a pan of water and something to eat by the time Sophia got home. Firewood was plentiful in and around Sea Breezes, and since Rich and Sophia's house had a fireplace, he had already filled a log rack with wood before the Collapse. As they started to burn the firewood for heating and cooking back in February he had cut off more limbs from the oak and pine trees they had in their front and back yards. The fire lighter they had used still had most of its propane, and they hadn't even started using the several boxes of matches they kept on hand.

Real coffee and real tea were long gone. All he had were some dried dandelion leaves to make a weak tea- but at least it would be hot. There was also some dried fish, a few MRE crackers, and one small tomato from the community garden. He hesitated to slice that scarce delicacy, but Sophia would be tired from her 8-hour shift on the roof in the northeast corner of the roughly rectangular Sea Breezes housing development. She would want something to eat and then get some sleep.

As he sipped his dandelion tea, he sat down and made some notes that he'd use when he addressed the neighbors at the picnic area up by the central lake. He wanted to run some of his thoughts by Josh Koenig, who was not only his brother-in law, but also a retired Marine Gunnery Sergeant with several years of combat experience himself.

There were just so many questions and "what-ifs" to be considered, and he admitted he certainly didn't have many answers. He hoped Josh would help him find some.

Chapter 2

Josh and Carmen Koenig were also up at first light in their two-story home near the Sea Breezes' entrance gate, not far from the community's lake. They, along with their young daughter, Nichole, were mirroring what Rich had done in putting together a morning meal. Their 16-year old son, Sean, was getting ready to go back on roof guard duty after an all too brief rest period, as his shift transitioned from afternoon to early morning duty.

They had just made some changes to the guard rosters now that it was summer time. Roof guard duty was now divided up into three unequal shifts: a morning shift from 6 a.m. to 2 p.m.; an afternoon shift, during the hottest part of the day, from 2 p.m. to 8 p.m.; and a night shift from 8 p.m. to 6 a.m. The shifts rotated time slots every two days so they could all have some time off during both days and nights. They had two sets of guards and they alternated duty every other week. The QRF teams were, by necessity, permanent assignments.

Each of the roof guards had a walkie-talkie, as did Rich and Josh. There had been a few pairs in the community when the Collapse came, but fortunately Sea Breezes got organized quickly and Rich made sure that on their early scavenging trips they scrounged more radios from Home Depot and various electronic stores. They even had a few spares. The radios stayed on station with each shift change.

Josh's main responsibility in the community was to manage the guard forces, from rooftop guards to the QRF team assignments, and adjust rosters when he had to find substitutes for people who were sick, hurt, or, in several instances already, killed. There were four QRF teams, each consisting of five men and women, with pre-designated rendezvous points in case of an attack. Each QRF team had a team leader.

After taking a lot of casualties in the continuing raids and attacks, Josh simply could no longer put together an able-bodied security force of adult men and women, so he was forced to lower the minimum age of the security forces to 16. He offered his son to be among the first children to be used for guard duty. He was completely confident in Sean's ability- he was a smart kid, and mature for his age. The family had enjoyed target shooting together before the Collapse, and Sean was very conscious of firearm safety. He was also a crack shot with his rifle.

Josh had an impressive collection of weapons. In fact, many of the guard forces' weapons were from his collection. Some of them were old, and truly collector's items, but he kept them all cleaned and in perfect working order. He had marked each rifle stock and pistol grip he loaned out to the guards with his initials, and made sure those he loaned the guns to understood he'd be looking to get them back when the crisis was over. He furled his brow as he had a disturbing afterthought, "If the crisis was ever over."

Over the past 24 hours, Josh and Carmen had been discussing the same thing everyone else in the community had: When can they expect some help from the force that landed? They also had stayed up last night talking about the situation and had the same doubts Rich had.

But they had decided not to burden their children this morning with their doubts, especially since Sean was scheduled to go back on duty as a roof top guard right after they ate something. Nichole was tasked to clean up the dishes after breakfast, while Carmen and Josh went into the living room to talk about their concerns.

Carmen looked at her husband and said, "So, it's not over yet is it, 'querido?'"

Josh shook his head, "No.... No it isn't, and not for a while, I think. We might get a little help at some point, if we're lucky, but can you imagine the work that has to be done? Just think- restoring water, electricity, food supply chains, government.... And that's assuming there are no more attacks from some group or country; and, that everyone cooperates. We may have discouraged China and Russia, and the Israelis made sure Iran won't be invading anyone soon, but that leaves a lot of bad actors out there. I hate to admit it, but the Navy saved our butts with their boomer subs, and they let everyone know not to screw with us. I do worry about the criminal elements, as well as jihadists. Those crazies won't ever give up, and they'll have to be dealt with at some point, along with everything else.

He paused a minute as his mind raced. "By the way, how are we doing on food?"

"Better than most, Josh. But all we have left are a few freeze dried cans of entrees and fruits and some MRE leftovers." She crinkled her eyes in a smile and said, "Those damn crackers will probably still be edible a hundred years from now."

Josh smiled in return, and changed the subject again. "Well, I'm glad you're helping out on the community garden out in Phase II, but with all of the wild animals gone, we'd better hope our fishermen bring in more fish from the Gulf. What we need is a bigger boat to get out into the deeper waters. I'll have to talk to Rich and see about finding us one or two somewhere.... Damn, there are just so many things to do."

Chapter 3

Sophia looked at her watch from her perch behind the sandbags on top of the roof of a neighbor's house. It was almost 6 a.m. and she looked around for her relief guard. No one was in sight.

It had been another long, boring night, trying to stay awake, but like the other guards, she took the role of guarding the community against attack seriously. It did give her some time to worry about what yesterday's landing force was going to do, and if they could expect any help from them. She and Rich had talked about it a few times, and had discussed it with a few of their neighbors. Some were very optimistic, but most, like Rich, were more doubtful.

Guards occasionally fell asleep on duty, and on one night before, that had undoubtedly cost the lives of some of their neighbors during the big attack by the Werewolves. After that, few roof guards did, although with the poor nutrition of everyone in the community, falling asleep still happened once in a while. The daylight guards had it easier- people passing by would holler up, "Hey, Brian, how you doin'?" "Hey, Barbara, how's it goin'?" So almost no one fell asleep during the day.

Night was different- all alone, scared, hungry, cold. Regular people, folks with no military training, had a hard time staying awake and focused. Sophia was tough as nails, though, and if she had to pinch herself or dig her nails into her thigh, she would never let herself fall asleep "on duty." She wasn't about to let Rich down.

At 6:15, her relief showed up. No apology was given for being a little late, and none was asked. A few brief words indicating nothing had happened on her shift, and she handed over the 5.56 mm rifle to her relief. The rifle was actually Rich's, but it stayed with the rooftop guards, 24/7. There just weren't enough rifles for every guard to have his or her own. She wearily climbed down the ladder on the side of the house, and headed home.

Sophia opened the front door at about 6:30. She was wearing blue jeans and a black long-sleeve T-shirt since it still got chilly in the evenings, especially up on the rooftops in the early morning sea breezes. It wasn't nearly as bad as the near-freezing temperatures of the previous winter of course, but not comfortable either. In fact, blankets that were used in the cold evenings of February and March to keep the roof guards warm were now being used to insulate the guards from the heat of the shingles on the hot June afternoons.

Rich looked up at her when she walked into the living room and thought, "My God, she's so thin. And she looks so tired." But she was still such a beautiful woman it made his heart ache to see her so exhausted. He got up and walked over to her and gave her a quick kiss.

"How'd it go, babes?"

She looked back at him as she headed into the kitchen to pour herself a cup of tea and answered over her shoulder, "Nothing happened. I didn't see any movement at all outside of the perimeter fence, not even from the occasional individual or small group we've seen in the past. I think the Zulus and what's left of the Werewolves were busy trying to figure out what they're going to do now that the cavalry has arrived."

She continued as she poured her tea, "I was thinking... they've got to know they're vulnerable out here on our little island with only one damaged bridge to get back to the mainland, and I doubt they're considering escaping by boats. They have to know that at some point down the road, law and order will be re-established, and after all the crimes and murders they've committed they'll be locked up, or worse. I was thinking that if I were them, I'd be planning on getting out of Dodge while I still can before I got trapped and couldn't escape."

"Yeah, that's one of the things I was thinking about last night too. I imagine some pretty heated discussions going on in both camps. The Zulus have still got to be pretty strong down there in Pelican's Landing. We took out five or six of them in that first attack against us, but even with that, along with their casualties from the inter-gang fights in the city, and maybe a few losses from their takeover of Pelican's Landing, they probably have two dozen or so fighters, and more hangers-on. I just hope they don't try to make one last raid on us before they go. I know we've got a tentative cease fire with them, but they're gangsters, and they may be getting desperate.

"I'm not worried too much about the remaining Werewolves at Sunset Beach- I bet they have less than a dozen fighters left after we ambushed them, and I don't think they want another taste of attacking us after we tore them up last time they tried."

Sophia was deep in thought for a few minutes, then looked up from her plate of dried fish at Rich and said, "Rich, really, when do you think the Army will come and rescue us? I mean, how much longer do we have to live like this?"

"Hon, honestly, I think it's going to be a while, maybe months. I've been thinking of all the other things the Army has to do here before they start worrying about rescuing communities. And remember, they have a lot bigger problems in the big cities and bases that got hit with the dirty bombs the terrorists set off. We're pretty small potatoes in the big scheme of things, and frankly, I'm surprised they came to Port Monroe as soon as they did. I guess they'd really like to get the port and the refinery operating again since we weren't hit by a dirty bomb, or they wouldn't be here at all. So in that sense we're lucky. So far we have no idea if these initial forces are going to stay. Among other things, sooner or later they've still got to clear that tanker hulk that was blown up near the port's entrance, and I doubt they have the equipment to do that themselves."

Sophia sighed, and said. "Rich it's just too much for me to think about right now, and it's depressing. I'm beat. I'm going to wash up and go to bed and try to get some sleep."

Rich noted she had left half of her meal on the plate, again. He wished she'd eat more, but she was so afraid of running out of food she often left part of a meal to save for the next one. "No wonder she's so thin," he thought. "I can't talk her into eating everything I put on her plate, so next time she leaves food, I will too. Maybe when she sees that she'll eat more."

He got up as she rose from the table, stepped over and hugged her close to him, and said, "Don't worry, honey. We've come this far and we'll figure something out, regardless of what happens. Go on up and hit the sack. I'm going to head up to Josh and Carmen's and talk to Josh to see what he thinks about the situation. Then we'll head on over to the daily nine o'clock meeting. Try to get some sleep." He bent down and kissed her as she headed upstairs, then he began to clear the table and wash the dishes in a pail of soapy water that they replaced every day.

Chapter 4

Rich went into the bathroom after he had cleaned up the kitchen, and with what little water was left in the same pail in the bathtub that Sophia had used, washed his face and hands. He peeked into the room to make sure Sophia was asleep. She was, lying there naked, as the sun's rays coming through the windows warmed the room, with her long black hair spread out over the pillow in the shape of a coral fan. He just stared at her for a few moments, suppressing his immediate desire, which he quickly dismissed as a selfish thought. He quietly shut the door, went to the utility room, grabbed a leash and hooked up Tasha, their Siberian Husky. The two then set out towards the lake and the Koenigs' house. The weather was already warm enough to be comfortable in just shorts and a t-shirt.

As he walked down the road he felt a light breeze ruffle his longish salt and pepper hair. His mind wandered and he thought about needing another haircut from Sophia soon. She had already told him she was cutting her long hair short since today ended her night shift. No way was she going to have long hair when she started the hot afternoon shift tomorrow. Plus, she said she was just tired of messing with it.

He realized that the limp from the horrible wound to his leg that he'd gotten on his last tour in Afghanistan didn't hurt as much as it used to. Funny how losing 20 pounds and getting more exercise helped reduce the pain. One thing about this whole ordeal was that very few people in Sea Breezes still carried much extra weight these days, and some were downright thin.

Tasha had also been wounded in an earlier raid on Sea Breezes, so she still limped a bit, even though she had lost a lot of weight also. Rich looked at her trotting ahead of him and thought, "Damn. Poor girl, just when I'd gotten her back to a normal weight after we rescued her, she now looks like she did when we picked her up." Tasha looked back at him as if she was reading his thoughts, and Rich would swear that she smiled. He did too.

A little before eight o'clock, Rich knocked on the Koenigs' door, which Carmen immediately opened. "Hey, Rich, we've been expecting you. Come on in. We've been talking about the situation and you and Josh need to get your heads together before the meeting. We're pretty confused as to what's going to happen next, and just what we need to be doing while we wait for some kind of help from the Army."

Rich stepped into the living room and Josh stood up and gave him a quick hug, with "Hey, 'hermano', how you doin'? How's my sister?"

"She's' fine, Josh, just really tired. Let's sit down and talk a bit. Carmen says you guys have been talking about what's next for us, and so have Sophia and I. I just hope that some of the rest of our neighbors have started thinking the situation through also, or there are going to be some pretty broken hearted people after today's meeting."

The daily meeting at the picnic area by the fenced-in lake in the center of the community had become a ritual, as did the weekly swap meets to exchange items people had found, made or grown. Some people just came to socialize and let their kids romp around together. The bazaars, as they called them, kept a semblance of normality to what was a horrible circumstance, and it helped all concerned keep up their morale.

After Josh and Rich talked for a while, they rewrote Rich's notes of important points to cover, and since they had about 20 minutes before the meeting Josh suggested they run by Donna Fleer's house to sound her out. Rich agreed, "Good idea, Josh, let's go."

Chapter 5

Donna was an attractive single woman in her 40's, and a former cop, who had been elected by the neighbors of Sea Breezes to serve as the "Judge" and arbitrator of the community. When the Collapse hit she was working for a security company, and at the time she had no steady boyfriend. Unfortunately, there hadn't been a lot of dating opportunities after the Collapse, and only two single men lived in Sea Breezes, Jacob Hanson and Bill Thornton, both of whom had since found partners in the community. Not that she had found either one of them tempting anyway.

In addition to Donna's appointment as judge, five jurors had also been nominated and elected. As a former cop she knew something about the law and she was a good fit for the job. The five jurors were respected members of the community.

They had already benefited from her trial skills on one occasion, when she had expelled a thief and slacker from the community. Donna had also proved to be an able fighter during the big night raid by the Werewolves. She had been the leader of one of the QRF teams, and had taken the lead in a counterattack that put the Werewolves on the run. She was a tough and smart woman who had become a respected leader in the community.

She was washing dishes when she heard someone knocking on her front door. She quickly grabbed a towel and dried her hands, then went to the front door. She smiled when she saw Rich and Josh. "Come on in guys, I was hoping you'd swing by here before the meeting. I've been meaning to talk to you both about our situation now, and about when you think we can expect to get some help from the Army."

"Well, Donna," said Rich, "we have a lot of questions, but we don't have any answers. I think we need to make some assumptions and best guesses, especially for the long run. Josh and I think that one of two different things is likely to happen over the next few months, but neither is a happy picture. I think we need to talk with the neighbors, and let them know that things aren't likely to be getting any better for us for some time to come. They deserve an honest explanation of what we think will likely happen. Josh and I made some notes of important points to cover." He held the notes out to her and she took them.

"Yeah, I was afraid of that. I hope some of the neighbors have already figured that out also. Let me see what you've got."

Donna scanned the notes, nodding her head, then she said to Josh, "I see you guys have been thinking about the guard problem also. It's getting damn hot during the day, and I'm glad you're thinking about doing something about that as soon as we get some relief.

"I'd like a few minutes to speak to our neighbors also after you guys finish. We can't let ourselves become demoralized, and we've got to maintain a sense of order and responsibility. Rich, why don't you lead off, and then Josh can talk about maybe being able to change our security posture at some point. Does that sound OK?"

Josh looked at Rich and said, "Yeah, that sounds good." He looked at his watch and said, "Well, it's almost 9, so let's head on up there."

When they arrived, nearly every man, woman and child in Sea Breezes, except for those on roof guard duty, were gathered around the picnic tables. There was an unusual amount of buzz as people were discussing, and in some cases arguing, about what was going to happen to the community in the next few weeks.

One man yelled out, "Hey, Rich, is it true we're gonna be rescued soon? Do you think they'll bring food in to us? Others were shouting questions also. "Josh can we quit having roof guards now?" "Hey, Donna, what are we going to do if some of the missing homeowners come back?" This from a man who had moved into a home that had been vacated because the couple who owned it had been on vacation up north somewhere when the attacks hit.

More questions were being shouted, so Rich stood up on a picnic table and called for quiet. The cacophony died down quickly and all eyes and ears were on him.

"Friends, it's a welcome sight to see that the Army has come to Port Monroe, but we've got to be realistic about what they're here for, and their primary mission is not going to be coming to rescue us." He then went on to discuss the sequence of events that he and Sophia, and later Josh and Donna, had discussed, emphasizing that the big question was whether the force that landed yesterday was a just a reconnaissance force or the advanced party to an occupation force.

"So, folks, nothing is going to change for us for some time yet." There were groans and even a few cries of anguish from the crowd. "As I mentioned though, the Werewolves, and especially the Zulus, have got to be thinking about clearing off the island soon, while they still can. And that may make us more vulnerable in the short run, since they may try to hit us and steal as much food and ammunition as they can before they take off. We can't let our guard down just yet, and we're still going to have to continue our foraging, hunting, and fishing sorties, and expand our gardening efforts.

"But we can do a few more things that will help us. Out in the abandoned Phase II area to the north of us, there are areas that are clear enough to make a sign and a helicopter landing pad among the poured foundations - you know, out there where we set up the firing range south of the marsh. We need to get everyone who has any white or light colored paint, to bring whatever you have to the entrance gate to Phase II, and help us gather up some large stones or bricks or whatever. We're going to build a 'HELP' sign and a helicopter landing pad so they can see it from the air. We need to let them know that there are some folks still alive here on the island, and that we need assistance. I'll head up that team, so bring your paint and rocks- nothing smaller than a brick so it won't get blown away. Load them up in wheelbarrows and bring them with you. I'll see you the back gate at 1 p.m."

Rich knew that giving them something positive to do would help reanimate their spirits a bit, although he knew that even if an aircraft were to fly over and see their message, it wouldn't mean they'd stop everything they were doing to come help.

"Now I'm going to turn the meeting over to Josh. He's got some changes in our security plans to go over. Josh?"

Rich gave Josh a hand up onto the top of the table and stepped down to listen. Josh began, "OK, we've still got the same threats out there that we've had for a while, but the good news is that we expect the gangs to hightail it back to the mainland at some point. But until they're gone, we've got to stay vigilant. Since the Zulus and the Werewolves took over large communities, they probably killed or drove out most of the residents, so hopefully they still have enough food left, but we have no way of knowing for sure. And regardless, they may want more, or they may want to take a stab at some payback against us, so we can't let our guard down- literally.

"So for now there will be no change in the QRF force or the roof guard rosters. In fact, we're going to have to set up a daylight two-man observation team to watch the bridge in case either of the gangs leave the island, and especially to be there if some Army vehicle should come to check things out here on the island. I doubt the latter will happen any time soon, but we can't afford not to know if they do come.

"I'll set up a new roster for the bridge observation team. I'll take a couple of guys out later this afternoon to find a nice hidden spot to observe the bridge from, and once we post lookouts there, they can stay in contact with me using one of the walkie-talkies. If anyone 16 or over who isn't already on rooftop guard duty wants to volunteer to be on one of those two-man teams, come see me after the meeting. I may have to go knocking on doors if I don't get enough volunteers. OK, any questions? If not, Donna would like to say a few words."

Josh helped Donna up onto the table, then he stepped down off to the side. Donna looked out at the crowd and started off with, "Look, I know all of this talk about having to wait longer for some relief or rescue is depressing to think about, but we do have some things we can do for ourselves until the time we make contact with the Army and start getting back to normal."

She paused, and continued, "Making the "HELP" sign and clearing a helicopter pad are just a couple of things we can do now. We've also got to keep up and expand our gardening efforts; and, we have to keep our bodies, homes, and neighborhood as clean as possible. I've noticed that some of the garbage and waste pits you all have dug in your yards are filling up. Some of you have already dug new ones, but it's time for the others to be covered up and new ones dug. You want at least three feet of dirt on top of your waste, so if you need to dig a new pit, get started on it now before it's too late.

"Please don't let tempers flare and get out of control. I don't want to have to have another trial because somebody did or said something stupid. We've got to keep it together for ourselves, our children, and our neighbors." She paused again and looked out at her neighbors and saw some heads nod and others looking down with tears in their eyes.

"I know the stress levels are high- none of us are used to living like this- but we can and will endure. We have endured- we are survivors. And for the record, I'm confident we will be rescued, I just don't know when. Until then, we have to stay strong and continue to help each other out. So, let's get to work."

Donna stepped down and the neighbors slowly melted away back towards their homes, some talking, some crying, others silently determined. She thought, "This isn't going to be easy."

Chapter 6

Among those who missed the morning meeting were Julia Reed and her new husband, Bill Thornton. Bill was a widower, and next-door neighbor, who had been helping Julia at the aid station. Julia was a nurse who had worked at the small hospital on the island, and was the only person in Sea Breezes with any medical training. She had established and run an aid station of sorts for the community in her house, and after a few months of close contact working with Bill, she moved in with him and his two kids.

Actually, Julia ran more than just an ordinary aid station. She had done a little of everything, including minor surgery and trying to patch up those who had been wounded. Thankfully, she had made sure that she went out on all the scavenging missions, and while others were looking for food and tools, she was looking for drugs, alcohol and first aid supplies. Thanks to a helpful nurse and doctor, she had even gotten a box full of more advanced medical instruments, scalpels, sutures, and hypodermic needles from the hospital just before it closed down. She often wondered what had happed to Dr. Rajan, the last doctor to abandon the hospital in the days after the Collapse.

Julia had been an OR nurse, and she was able to remove bullets, and clean and suture wounds herself. But there hadn't been any large-scale attacks recently, and more of her "patients" came for treatment of illnesses such as diarrhea, colds or the flu, or broken bones, and other minor medical problems. Bill and his two children were a big help. Bill's 16-year old son, Wayne, was now on the guard force. In fact he was on the same rooftop guard shift as his young friend, Sean Koenig. But Bill's young daughter, Nichole, had learned to be a pretty damn good nurse under her tutelage.

The reason neither Julia nor Bill went to the meeting was because of two young children brought in by their mother for treatment this morning. The young boy and girl were running fevers and had severe, watery diarrhea. The problem was, both children had been in two days before and, thinking it was just run of the mill GI upset, she had given them both Imodium tablets and plenty of water. But they were back today, and their symptoms were worse.

Julia left the bedroom the kids were in with their mom, and pulled Bill out with her into what used to be her living room and was now the waiting room/reception area. "Bill, I'm afraid those kids have Cholera. I've been worried about Cholera showing up now for weeks. We get some of our water from ground water and irrigation wells, and I think that fecal contamination has gotten into some of the ground water we use. Kids and older folks are more susceptible, and I think that's what these kids have. Without a lab, I don't have any way to tell for sure, but we've got to assume the worst. Cholera spread through contaminated water, so I'm going to have to assume that that is what it is. We need to alert the community to start boiling any water they take out of or off the ground. We've been fortunate that it's rained enough for people to collect rainwater for a lot of our needs, but groundwater has got to always be boiled from now on."

Bill listened quietly and asked, "How bad is it? Do we need to quarantine the kids and their family?"

"Yes, and right away and for at least 10 days after the kids recover. We can't have them playing with other kids or even being near them until they've fully recovered. The disease also spreads by saliva. Cholera works fast and if we hadn't treated the kids day before yesterday they might not be alive now, what with everyone's body so weak. I have some Pedialyte to give them, but with Cholera we don't really want to stop the diarrhea so no more Imodium. We've got to nip this in the bud right away."

She glanced out the window and saw some people walking back from the lake and said, "I see today's meeting has already broken up. I'll walk up and let Donna know about the Cholera and she can tell everyone at tomorrow's meeting. I don't remember who came up with the idea of having daily meetings, but I sure am glad they did.

"In the meantime, we can probably expect more cases to come in, since Cholera can take up to five days before symptoms occur. Let's go tell the mom so she can take her kids home and keep them there- and she needs to stay away from other folks for 10 days also."

Bill said, "OK. I'm going to go out and ask one of our neighbors to find out what went on at the meeting. See you in a few minutes."

Chapter 7

Leroy Ivory and his wife, Althea, were two of the people who had moved into the neighborhood after the Collapse. Leroy was a retired Marine Gunnery Sergeant, and had fought in Vietnam when he was a young man. He used to run a nearby gas station convenience store, and had become friends with Josh. The Ivorys had been rescued by Josh and Rich from their home a few miles away and were brought into Sea Breezes to live in a vacant house. A few people were on vacation when the Collapse came, and others never returned from work on the day the oil refinery blew up, so there were a few houses in Sea Breezes that were vacant. Leroy had been a great addition to the guard force, and he had led the ambush party that had decimated the Werewolves. Althea had also been contributing to the community by working in the community garden and by helping Julia at the aid station when there was a flood of sick or wounded.

Leroy was on one of the QRF teams and he decided he'd volunteer to be one of the observers at the bridge. He knew how to hide, observe, and communicate, and wouldn't mind spending the daylight hours on bridge observation duty. After the meeting broke up he caught up with Josh.

"Hey, Josh, wait up. Listen, I'll sign up for that bridge duty. I'm not doing anything but serving on a QRF team, and there's no reason I can't do both, since the QRF is only deployed when we're attacked. And I don't think we need a roster. Sitting and observing isn't much work, so find me a partner and we can do the job every day."

Josh grinned at his friend and said, "Thanks, Leroy. I think someone with your experience is just what we need. I'll get another "volunteer" one way or another, so let's meet at my house at one o'clock and the three of us can head out in my truck to look for a good hiding and observation point near the bridge."

The two friends chatted for a few minutes, and Leroy was about to leave when he saw a boy walking towards them. It was Malcolm Brown, the oldest son of recently widowed Kathryn Brown's three children. Malcolm's father was one of those who never made it home after the oil refinery blew up and burned.

Kathryn was a strong and determined woman, and one of the hardest workers in the community. She was lithe but strong and worked in the community garden. She also did whatever other small tasks for the community she could help with. Everyone was surprised when she allowed her son to go on roof guard duty, but she felt it was her family's obligation to help provide security for the community, and single parents were not allowed to go out on scavenging trips or pull guard duty.

When Malcolm got to the two men he said, "Josh, I'd like to volunteer for the bridge duty. I need a change from being a roof guard, and I think my mom is getting worried about me being up on a roof all alone."

Josh looked over at Leroy, but saw no reaction so he asked, "Malcolm, how old are you?" Malcolm stood up straight and said, "I'm 16, and I know how to shoot. My dad taught me." Josh looked over at Leroy, who nodded his approval, then said, "Sure, Malcolm. Meet us at my house at one and we'll go scout out a location where we can set up."

Leroy said, "OK, Malcolm, it looks like we're a two-man team. He smiled at the young man and added, "We'll guard the bridge like that Roman, Horatio." Malcolm got a puzzled look on his face so Leroy explained, "I'll tell the story of Horatio to you later. It'll give us something to talk about. By the way, what kind of gun do you have?"

"Mr. Ivory, all I've got is a pistol my mom borrowed from Mr. Cantrell."

Josh said, "Well I guess I'm going to have to find you a rifle to take along with you also. In case something happens it's likely to begin at some distance. But bring your pistol along too."

Leroy had a Colt .45 semi-auto that Josh had loaned him, and his own shotgun, which he knew would come in handy if the shit hit the fan. Leroy put his hand on Malcolm's shoulder and said "I'll see you later, partner." Malcolm grinned and said, "You bet, Mr. Ivory."

As Josh walked away, he grinned and again said to himself, "Huh. An old Marine and a young man, on the same team. Maybe they'll both learn something. Anyway, that was easy. One less thing I have to get done."

Chapter 8

Rich was at the back gate precisely at one o'clock, and there were several men and women already there, with paint cans and a wheelbarrow full of paving stones. He waited another 15 minutes and a few more people showed up with spray paint and house paint, in shades of yellow, beige, and white, and another came with a wheelbarrow full of big rocks that he'd scrounged.

Rich looked at everyone, nodded approvingly and said, "Let's go. I know a couple of areas that will be good for the 'HELP' sign and the helicopter pad." He headed north followed by a trail of neighbors lined up with their loads, like ducklings behind a mamma duck.

When he got out to a cleared area just on the south side of where the marsh started, he stopped and said, "OK. We're going to first make a large 'HELP' sign right here. The letters need to be about six feet high, so let's start lining up rocks to form an "H." Those of you who just brought paint spread out and find some big rocks and bring them back here."

Everyone did as Rich said, and pretty soon they had spelled out the word "HELP" in big capital letters. Rich then grabbed a couple of spray cans of white paint and started painting the rocks for the "H". Others started painting the rest of the letters with various light colors until the work was complete.

Rich stood back and said, "Well, that looks pretty good. Now let's go over there", he pointed at a large concrete foundation that had been poured for a house that was never started and said, "We'll paint a big 'H' in the center of that concrete foundation and draw a big circle around the 'H'. That will indicate to a helicopter pilot that someone on the ground knows the area to be clear for the helicopter blades and that the landing pad is stable enough so that a helicopter can land there. Make the 'H' about 6 feet tall."

Kathryn Brown had a piece of chalk and she outlined a perfect letter "H." Then she took a can of yellow paint and and carefully painted a four inch wide letter "H" over the chalk markings, and the job was done. Another neighbor took the last can of spray paint and made a big white circle around the "H." Kathryn turned to look at Rich with a grin on her face and said, "How's that?"

Rich said, "That looks great, Kathryn. Mission accomplished. Now, there's one last thing that we need to do." He pulled a 6 ft. American flag out of his backpack and held it up for everyone to see.

"We're going to raise this flag out here for several reasons. First it will attract attention, and hopefully it will also indicate that we are the good guys. And, it will also serve as a wind sock for any chopper that tries to come in to land. The sea breezes can be tricky, and this will be some help any pilot who tries to land- not as good as a real wind sock, but better than nothing. I need a volunteer to run back to my house and pick up the long flagpole that used to be in Josh's front yard. Josh and I dug it up before we came out here, and I carried it home with me and put it in my back yard."

Wayne Thornton, Bill and Julia's son, half raised his hand and said, "I'll do it!" He didn't wait for any acknowledgement. He just took off running. A few minutes later he was back carrying a 15 ft. flagpole. While he was gone, Rich took a garden spade out of his backpack and walked about 35 yards east of the helicopter landing pad, right above their big "HELP" sign in the dirt. He started digging a narrow hole the length of his hand and forearm, and turned around just as Wayne returned with the flagpole and set it down beside him. He looked at the boy, grinned, and said, "Good timing, Wayne. Next thing, everybody go pick up some small rocks, from pebbles to walnut size."

As people scurried around hunting rocks, Rich said to Wayne, "Son, pick up the end of the flagpole and slide down about 8 ft. and hold it up so I can hook on the flag." Once the flag was hooked on, Rich and Wayne raised the pole and set it in the hole. Several people had come back with small rocks and he told them to dump them around the flagpole's base. They did so until the hole was filled, and Rich had been adding dirt along the way. Rich took his canteen out and watered the hole, and kept adding dirt until the dirt and rocks were tightly packed, He then grabbed a few of the leftover paving stones and stacked them around the pole to help steady it if a strong wind came up.

He stepped back and looked up at the flag, as did the others. He said, "Well, this may not exactly be an Iwo Jima moment, but the Stars and Stripes sure looks good up there." Those that understood the reference smiled. A couple of the men even saluted along with Rich, and the happy crowd trudged back towards the back gate. They all felt that they had at least done something to improve their chances for getting some help from the Army.

Rich knew that Phelps Island wasn't on the aircraft approaches to the airport, but maybe a scout helicopter might get close enough to see the sign. He just wondered if the Army had the time and resources to do anything about it.

Chapter 9

While the residents of Sea Breezes were engaged in the simple task of making a "HELP" sign, the president of the United States was at Camp David, waiting in his office before entering the conference room for his first fully-attended staff meeting since the Collapse.

He and his acting staff had moved just a week ago from their underground bunker in West Virginia to Camp David because there already existed a complete above ground facility as well as a sophisticated communication array, recently enhanced by equipment from the military bases around Washington D.C. It would be months before the White House and all the government headquarters in Foggy Bottom were decontaminated and available to occupy again.

His staff had been scattered across the country on the day of the attack, and several didn't survive the devastation of those first few days. In those cases, the president had elevated the next senior official available to the top position, and some of those had been the ones he was able to round up before he was evacuated from the White House. Some of his primary staff members were now men and women three levels down from the missing heads and deputies.

As the principals and staff trickled in from around the country, they had simply outgrown the emergency facilities. Camp David was crowded also, and some staffers were living in temporary tents and plywood shelters. But everyone they could account for were now in place in one location.

The president looked at his watch- five minutes to go before he would walk into the meeting. He had been thinking that no other American president had ever had such a difficult and challenging crisis to deal with- not even president Lincoln or his successor, president Johnson, faced the kind of devastated country after the Civil War that he was facing today. But, all things considered, he thought things were going as well as could be expected.

Precisely at 1 p.m., he walked into the conference room and all rose. "Please be seated, ladies and gentlemen." He took his seat at the head of the table, and continued, "A few of you are here for the first time since the Collapse, and I've been dealing with your deputies on a daily basis up until now. I have to say that everyone has performed admirably, but it's nice to have a full staff again, all in one location. I can tell you that there is not a more secure few square miles anywhere on the planet than where we are right now." That brought some smiles to the men and women in the room, and they all relaxed a bit.

"Up until now we've been more reactive than proactive, but as far as security is concerned, we are doing fantastically well. We've set China, Russia, and Iran back on their heels with our combined non-nuclear and cyber attacks, and they understand that any further hostile actions towards us on their part will be met with a devastating nuclear onslaught. Thank God for our submarine fleet- they are within striking distance of all of our enemies as we speak, and our enemies know I'm not afraid to retaliate and even escalate if I have to. Of course, they have as many problems as we do, and fewer resources to work with. We may be down, but we're not out by a long shot.

"We've brought home all of our armed forces from overseas, along with all of their supplies and as much of their equipment as we could move, and put them to work inside the United States. We have aircraft and trucks, and the people to maintain them; but, we have few supplies to transport. We have to put our emphasis on consolidating our national reserves and our foreign aid and get supplies, especially food, out to all areas. Our traditional allies that weren't attacked have proven to be loyal, and I have personally thanked each president, chancellor and premier who has helped us. Those allies in Europe who were attacked are struggling as much as we are.

"Pulling out all of our combat forces has destabilized parts of the world, and only the threat of our nuclear submarines are keeping our enemies at bay. But the Middle East has declined into a tribal and religious conflagration, and they'll just have to sort things out for themselves now.

"I want to establish some other priorities, now that I am fairly confident of our national security, at least as far as danger from further attacks from abroad. I need a progress report from the Department of Homeland Security and FEMA on the status of our effort to reconstitute our coastal and internal transportation hubs and economic infrastructure as well as the status of the refugee camps we established outside the cities and military bases that were hit with the dirty nuclear bombs. These, of course, are the critical targets selected by the Islamic terrorists to cripple us, and we must either get them functioning again or we need to look for smaller areas that weren't hit that we can get up to speed quicker. I'm talking about military bases, ports, refineries, storage facilities, and everything having to do with the production of food, from farming to baking and butchering. And, of course a transportation and distribution network for getting the final products out to hurting Americans.

"We know the countryside is much better off than the large cities, and that many cities of all sizes have been for all intents and purposes, depopulated. We simply were not able to establish refugee camps for all of them, so we had the difficult task of picking those cities that are of most importance to our national security and our economic recovery. The hardest task I have ever had to do personally as president was to make the horrible decision to abandon certain cities in favor of those that can be reconstituted rapidly. But I need a timeline on when we'll be able to start assisting those areas that we've had to leave to their own fate.

"I need to get an update from the FCC on restoring our national radio and TV networks. I know we've reestablished communications in and around our larger cities and military bases, but I'm concerned about getting the word out to all of our citizens in the smaller cities and the heartland, where there are survivors clinging to existence. I want a coverage map that shows what areas are covered by radio, and which are covered by TV. In those areas where we have no radio coverage, I want to make sure there's a priority of resources for those areas before we expend any more effort on expanding television coverage.

"You all have been asked to prepare a no more than 10-minute briefing to us all- and I emphasize the 'brief' part of that word- on what the status is of your particular areas of responsibility, and what you need from other departments and agencies to do your jobs. After today's staff meeting, another 15 minutes have been allotted to each of you privately with me for the rest of the afternoon and evening. At the end of this meeting we'll begin the one-on-one meetings and go until we take a break for dinner at 6 p.m. Then, we'll start up again at 7 p.m. SECDEF (Secretary of Defense) you're up first on the schedule, as you know.

"As each of you begin your 10-minute briefing to all of us, I want to emphasize to everyone here to make sure that coordination and cooperation among agencies is facilitated, and although I'm confident that at this level we have that, make sure your subordinates know this also. Coordination and cooperation are essential. I don't want any answers that start with "We can't." What I want to happen is for an answer to be "Let's see how we can get this done together." There will be no turf battles or interagency strife. Tell your people that if they can't cooperate, I will fire them and replace them with someone who will.

"Last thing. I know you have all worked tirelessly with very few days off. But you're no good to me if you're walking around like a zombie. Take care of yourselves, and make sure your people do too.

You all have been truly outstanding so far, and I am grateful to you each and every one of you. The president looked around the room at every person in the room, smiled and said, "Let's put America back together again."

Chapter 10

As the president was opening his first full staff meeting at Camp David, Leroy and Malcolm showed up at Josh's house right at one o'clock. They piled into his truck and headed towards the bridge, with Leroy in the pickup bed and the other two in the cab. Josh said, "Both of you keep your eyes peeled and if you see anything move before I do let me know. We're out in Indian country now, and I want to avoid a run-in with hostiles if we possibly can. I don't expect any traffic heading towards the bridge, or from the city, but you never know, so keep a lookout. Leroy, you keep an eye on our back trail. Malcolm, you look to the front and sides with me as I drive." For Malcolm's sake, he added, "Keep your weapons pointed outwards in the direction you're looking."

Leroy said, "OK, I got our six." and Josh drove out of the entrance to Sea Breezes and headed south towards the east-west running Beach Parkway, where he hung a left towards the bridge.

To the left and right of him there were abandoned stores and the occasional small strip mall. Some vehicles were parked in the lots, never to be picked up by their owners. All of the stores and shops had been looted- there was no reason to stop and search places on this main road.

Josh kept up a steady 35 mph until they got within sight of the bridge. As they got near, Malcolm pointed to a strip mall on the right and said, "How about over there, in one of those buildings in that strip mall?"

The strip mall had only five stores in it. One of them was a coffee shop with big windows, one of which had been broken out. Josh smiled and said, "Looks like somebody had a real caffeine Jones going. I guess we won't have to worry about anyone showing up to buy coffee."

The shop was about 50 yards from the bridge, but it did have a clear view of the road coming towards the bridge, as well as of the bridge itself. Josh drove into the small parking lot, and said, "Well at least you'll be out of the sun, and it's pretty dark in there. Stay back away from the window and even if someone does drive by they won't see you unless you want to be seen. Leroy, what do you think?"

Leroy turned to Josh and said, "Looks as good as any other place, so let's plan on staying here. I can park a car around back, out of sight, and we can sit in there and watch and wait. Let's go take a look inside."

Josh pulled his truck around back, out of sight behind the stores, and parked it. The back door to the coffee shop was locked, so instead of trying to break the lock, they just walked around to the front and stepped through the broken widow. They checked quickly to make sure the place was clear and that there were no surprises. The place had been ransacked, but Leroy set up a couple of chairs and a table a few feet from the broken window, and said, "I think this will do."

The three of them checked out the shop quickly to see if there was anything useful, then unlocked the back door of the shop and headed back to the truck. Leroy looked at Josh and said, "If we see anything moving off the island, I'll radio you and let you know. If someone is coming in I'll let you know that too, but if it's a military vehicle, I'll go out and stop it while Malcolm radios you and then covers me. Does that sound OK?"

Josh said, "Sounds good to me. Let's start tomorrow." Both Leroy and Malcolm nodded agreement, so Josh turned the truck around and headed back to Sea Breezes.

As they approached the intersection to turn right on the road back into Sea Breezes, they heard the sound of a rifle firing and at the same time the windshield shattered. Josh was fleetingly distracted as he noticed the bullet running the width of the windshield as if was trying to zip it open. He immediately drove off into the ditch on the right-hand side of the road and hollered, "Get out, get out!"

Leroy and Malcolm bailed out of the truck out the passenger side and Josh ducked low and rolled out the bottom of the driver's side door, crawled under the truck, and joined the other two. "You guys OK? Anyone hit?" Malcolm shook his head no, but all they heard from Leroy was the sound of two quick booms from his shotgun. Malcolm looked under the car and saw movement and began firing his rifle also.

Josh pulled his pistol out and yelled, "What do you see, Leroy?"

Leroy said, "One guy over there behind the big tree on the opposite corner." Josh, you and Malcolm keep firing and keep his head down. I'll cross the road and try to come up on his left side."

Josh started firing along with Malcolm and yelled, "Go, go!" The man across the road popped up when he saw Leroy's motion to get a shot at him, but for some reason didn't shoot. Just then, the man caught a round in the shoulder from Malcolm's rifle. He screamed in pain and fell back. Then as he tried to scramble back up behind the tree, Leroy hit him in the arm on the same side with buckshot, and the man twisted backward and lay still. Leroy hit the ground, in case there was another shooter, but there was nothing but silence.

Josh said to Malcolm, "Cover me." and crawled up onto the road to take a look. He motioned to Leroy and they got up in a crouch, weapons pointed, and walked in a slow, low crouch towards the big tree. No one fired on them. When they got there, a thin, young black man, a boy, really, was on his back moaning. Leroy got to him first, looked around and then said, "Who the hell are you?"

The young man was moaning on the ground and he looked up, scared, and in pain, and said, "Help, me, man. Please! Oh God, it hurts." There were tears running down his face and Leroy answered, "Listen, bro, you tried to kill us, so don't be cryin' because we shot back. Tell us who you are and what you're doing here."

In between grimaces of pain, the young man said, "My name's Dante. I'm with the Zulus. They put me out here to watch for anythin' coming from Sea Breezes. If I see anythin' I'm s'pose to call back and tell them."

Leroy looked at him like he was stupid and said, "Jesus, bro, then why the hell did you shoot at us?"

Dante replied, "You wasn't coming from Sea Breezes, you were going into it." As if that explained it.

Josh shook his head and said, "Leroy, I think the kid fell asleep and didn't see us leave. I guess he heard us coming back and decided he should shoot. Dumbass."

Leroy said, "Aw, hell, Josh. What are we going to do with him? We can't just leave him here. I think we have to take him back with us and have Julia look at him.

Josh thought a second, and said, "Yeah, I guess that's what we have to do. I don't like it though." He turned to Dante and said, "When are they supposed to come pick you up?"

Dante was breathing hard, but managed, "As soon as it starts to get dark. They come down the road, turn around, and I'm s'pose to hop in whatever car or truck they send for me. We don't keep a watch at night. We know you people don't go out after dark."

Josh said, "Well that makes sense. Let's get him into the back of the pickup, and you can ride back with him. But first, check him out for weapons."

Leroy told Malcolm to keep his rifle trained on Dante while he patted him down and searched his pockets. All he found was some chewing gum, a spare 30-round magazine for his 5.56 mm rifle, and a flip knife, all of which he pocketed. He asked the young man, "How old are you, son."

Dante answered, "Seventeen. I ain't been with the Zulus 'til they took over our neighborhood, so I had to go along with them. Some of the things they done to those men and women in Pelican's Landing made me sick. I think that's why they stuck me out here."

Leroy shook his head, then took the young man's feet and told Malcolm to grab him under the arms. As Malcolm lifted him up Dante screamed loudly from the pain of the wounds to his shoulder. Leroy noticed that he was also bleeding from his side, so a pellet or two of buckshot must have got him there also. They lifted him into the bed of the pickup and Leroy climbed in behind Dante to keep an eye on him.

Josh looked around and found a walkie-talkie behind the tree and went over and pocketed it. He also picked up the kid's rifle, looked in the chamber, and noticed a shell casing stuck in the breech. He walked over to Leroy, and showed him the rifle. "Kid's rifle had a failure to eject the shell casing. That's why he didn't shoot your ass, old man. He probably didn't know how to clear it. And the rifle is rusty and dirty. I guess the Zulus aren't much into firearm maintenance."

Leroy just shook his head again, and Josh and Malcolm got back in the truck's cab. Josh pulled slowly back onto to the road and turned right on the road back to Sea Breezes.

They headed straight for the aid station and when they got there Malcolm ran in to get Julia. He came back out with her and Bill, who was carrying an improvised stretcher under his arm. Josh and Leroy picked up Dante and lay him on the stretcher, then Malcolm and Bill carried him inside.

They laid him on the dining room table that served as Julia's operating table. The kid had lost a lot of blood already, and he had passed out somewhere between the truck bed and the table.

"Jesus!" Julia exclaimed when she saw the kid's wounds. "Bill, help me cut off his shirt and I'll see what I can do. She looked him over and said to Leroy, "He's really lost a lot of blood, and I can't replace it. I can try to clean his wounds and sew him up, but I doubt he'll make it."

Leroy put his hands to his face, rubbed his eyes and said, "Well, do what you can, Julia. I'll stay with you in case he comes to. I want to make sure he's not going to say something else we could use, and make sure he doesn't wake up and become a threat. He looked down at Dante, shook his head, and said, "What a goddam shame."

He turned to Josh and said, "Josh, I was able to ask a few questions of Dante as we were riding back here. He said the Zulus were living high on the hog, with lots of booze, and there were about 35 of them in all, but only 20-25 or so adults who could shoot."

Josh nodded and said, "Well that's not as many as I feared, but still a force to be reckoned with. Let's go down to Rich's house and brief him on what happened." They went out the front door as Julia and Bill were cleaning off the blood around Dante's wounds.

Chapter 11

After Rich had heard Josh and Leroy tell their story, he started to say something and then stopped. "Wait a minute. Did you say the kid said they were living high on the hog?" Both men nodded, and Rich continued, "That may mean they really don't need to risk hitting us before they leave the island. And maybe we could discourage them further by taking out a few more of their fighters. I'm not looking for trouble but these gangs are utterly ruthless, and taking as many off the board as we can has got to be a good thing for everyone. What do you guys think about setting up another ambush for the Zulu's vehicle when it comes to pick up Dante? Depending on how many other observers they have out that they have to collect at dusk, we might take two or more of them out. It would be a pretty low risk operation too."

Josh and Leroy looked at each other, and Leroy said, "Yeah, that would work." He thought a few seconds and said, "Dante had on camouflage pants and a black T-shirt, and I have both at home that I could put on. Hell, I could put on Dante's cap too. Even if they couldn't reach the kid on his walkie-talkie, they would come check the situation out anyway.

He paused, thinking, and said, "Josh, give me the kid's radio. They may have arranged a time to check in, and if their base calls, I could just click the talk button off and on and let the breaking squelch sound as if the thing wasn't transmitting. They'd have to come and check out what happened, and if they hesitated when they didn't see Dante, I could step out into the road and wave. They're expecting to see a Black man in his cammie trou, black T-shirt and a cap, and that's what they'll see. I could take one of the QRF teams out there a couple of hours before dusk and set them up in a L-shaped ambush. Then when the Zulus get close enough, I'll run back and jump into the ditch and the ambush could open up on 'em. What do you think?"

Josh smiled at Leroy's excitement and looked over at Rich. Rich shrugged his shoulders and said, "Why not? The plan sounds solid and I don't see much risk to us. Let's do it. Josh, pick a QRF team and get them ready to go. We'll head out around 7 p.m., and get set up well before the sun sets. Once the car or truck is within range, we'll spring the ambush on Leroy's signal. Let's meet at Josh's house at 6:30 and lay out our plan to everyone."

Josh and Leroy both said, "OK" and headed off to get ready.

Chapter 12

Josh picked Donna's QRF team, and the four men and women with her, along with Josh, Leroy and Rich, piled into Josh's and Leroy's pickups. Leroy was dressed exactly like Dante had been- except he had a cleaned and well-oiled AR-15.

They drove back to the Beach Parkway intersection and Donna spread her team lengthwise in the trees along the length of Beach Parkway. Josh and Rich, along with Leroy, were the "L" along Sea Breezes Rd. They settled down, got comfortable, and watched.

Leroy had gotten one call for Dante from someone at their base, wanting to know if anything was going on. He answered by clicking the talk button on and off so there was just the sound breaking squelch, no voice transmission. He heard a response, "Hey Dante, your radio ain't transmitting. Break squelch twice if you hear me."

Leroy keyed the talk button twice, and the caller said, "OK, we'll be there in about fifteen." Leroy pressed the talk button twice again, to acknowledge. He shouted out to the QRF team, "Fifteen minutes. Get ready."

Twelve minutes later, they saw a pickup truck coming down Beach Parkway. It had what looked like a driver, a passenger riding shotgun, and one man sitting in the truck's bed. The truck slowed down as it neared the intersection but didn't stop. Leroy stepped out to the side of the road and waved his arm. As the truck got closer, Leroy decided he'd better not wait for them to get a good look at him so he dove into the ditch. When he did, the QRF team, Rich, and Josh opened fire. Leroy watched for about ten seconds and started hollering, "Cease fire! Cease fire!"

The QRF team was disciplined and did so immediately after hearing the command. Donna walked out and approached the truck carefully, her shotgun leveled at her cheek as she scanned the pickup. No one was moving. She lowered the shotgun and drew her pistol and checked each man carefully. Each one of them had multiple wounds, and all were dead from the overwhelming firepower.

Donna yelled out, "All Clear." The rest of her team approached, took a quick look, and stepped back to the side of the road. Rich, Leroy, and Josh searched the men, took their weapons, ammo, walkie-talkie, and a couple of candy bars, of all things, and pocketed them.

Rich looked at the other two and said, "You know, I'm tempted to stay here and wait for another of their vehicles to come check on what happened to this one, but, that could be a little dangerous, since they're bound to be more careful next time. This was easy, but I'd like to avoid a fight that might put some of our people at risk."

Josh said, "Yeah, it's tempting, but I agree." Leroy just said "Yup." Rich pulled out a piece of paper he had written on in black magic marker and a roll of scotch tape and taped the sign on the inside of the windshield. It said,

STAY AWAY FROM SEA BREEZES

AND GET OFF OUR ISLAND!

Everyone crowded around to read the sign Rich had put up. A couple of them laughed and one said "Hoo-Ahh!" Then they all walked back to the pickup, got in, and drove back to Sea Breezes.

Chapter 13

Every adult who was physically able, and not a sole parent, had rooftop guard duty except for Julia. It was a thankless, boring, uncomfortable task that everyone also knew had saved them from many attacks, including two big ones by the Werewolves and the Zulus. Even the former HOA president, Fred Carlucci, reluctantly pulled duty on the roofs. But he was still unhappy that he had lost the election to Donna to be the community's "Judge" and de facto community leader. He had opposed just about everything Rich and Donna had tried to do, but in the end he'd cooperated. If he didn't, he knew he'd be banished. They had already banished a guy by the name of Gary Holmes for stealing, and failing to show up for the QRF team that deployed one night during an attack. No one got to slack off in this community.

But he was angry that he wasn't getting enough to eat, and believed that other people in the community were hoarding food. He was always snooping around trying to discover someone eating more than the others. As a result, most people avoided him.

Fred's wife, Sheryl, was a small mousey-looking 67 year-old woman who never said much and just did what Fred told her to do. She was a worker in the garden, and didn't mind getting her hands dirty, literally, planting and weeding, but she couldn't work for long periods without stopping to rest.

She was one of the few adults who got a pass on pulling guard duty, because she was extremely weak from arthritis and a heart condition and, like so many others, malnutrition.

She and Fred had moved down from New York City after Fred had retired from the NYC public school system, and their one child was grown up and presumably still in New York- if he was alive, which Sheryl very much doubted. Like some of the other neighbors in Sea Breezes, she had pretty much given up hope and was just going through the motions of living.

The garden was doing OK, but the "Garden Club" as the members of the garden workers called themselves, just didn't have enough seeds on hand to make a big enough garden to feed the entire community. Produce was strictly rationed and the northern rooftop guard nearest the garden was told to keep an eye out for thieves- from both within as as well as outside of the community.

A few of the residents were fortunate enough to have planted orange or grapefruit trees in their yards, and most of them bartered some of the fruit from their trees at the weekly "bazaars." Some good souls gave fruit to neighbors who were in real need. The same held true for the few people who already had small gardens in their yards before the Collapse.

But it just wasn't enough.

Chapter 14

At the next morning meeting by the lake, Josh told the community about the bridge observers, the attack by a lone Zulu, and the ambush of the Zulus that followed. He again warned the roof guards to stay alert in case of retaliation.

Rich told everyone about the "HELP" sign they had laid out, making the helicopter pad, and the raising of the flag. He also reminded them that Sea Breezes wasn't along the normal flight paths in and out of Port Monroe's airport, and that even if some plane or helicopter did see the sign, they may not have the mission of rescuing civilians yet. "But," he said, "If you see an aircraft pass nearby it wouldn't hurt to stop what you're doing and wave your arms to try to get noticed. Maybe some pilot might take pity on us and when he got back, ask his boss to give us some help. Whatever you do, though, do NOT fire your weapons to get their attention. They might think you're firing at them and avoid us, or worse, fire back."

Julia told everyone about the suspected Cholera cases, and went over the strict measures people should follow to prevent becoming infected.

"Cholera can best be prevented, and cured, by drinking lots of clean, boiled water. Boil drinking water for at least five minutes. And if you come down with diarrhea, stay indoors except to dump your waste in your trash pits. And remember, we've to assume now that all groundwater is contaminated with Cholera. So next time we don't get enough rain and we have to use a generator to run an irrigation well for water, don't drink it, wash dishes in it, or bathe in it until it's been treated."

Josh came up next and said, "One thing I forgot to mention. We need to make a gas run today. So all pickups line up at my house at one and we'll head out."

All of the abandoned cars near Sea Breezes had long ago had their tanks siphoned, and the small portable generators they had wouldn't run the gas pumps. One of the neighbors, Jacob Hanson, was a plumber by trade, and had rigged up an irrigation pump, generator, and the nozzle and hose taken off a gas pump, so they could pump gas out the underground gas storage tanks of filling stations. There were several types of locks owners used to secure their underground tanks from theft. Leroy's old stop and shop had been burned by looters, but he had recently gone back through the burned out ruins and recovered his underground gas tank key and unlocking wrench.

The Sea Breezes residents didn't use that much gas- about the only times they went out of the community were for scavenging trips and they never went out very far. They used their generators sparingly, mostly for running an irrigation system with a hose valve diversion so they could fill their water buckets and at the same time, charge any rechargeable batteries they had. The aid station kept one for night emergencies and checking on critical patients after dark.

So far they had only had to go out once to get gas, but Josh knew they had better top off their vehicles soon, just to be safe. Trucks got priority, because they could haul more people and stuff, including the gas containers they had. Not that there was that much more stuff to be found, but they knew they still had to try. Food was critically low because the gardens, fruit trees and seafood, plus the occasional goose or other bird, just didn't supply enough to the community. Part of the reason for the top-off was that Josh knew they'd be going out scavenging again soon, and he also knew they'd have to risk going further out into areas they hadn't been to yet.

Fortunately, the two gangs that had taken up residence on the island had plenty of food from the two gated communities they had taken over. At least so far, neither of the gangs had bothered them on their scavenging trips. There was only that first time when some rednecks in two pickups jumped them while they were loading up material from the Home Depot nearby. There was some danger from some of the smaller bands of raiders that were pillaging around the island, but they had already tested Sea Breezes' defenses on a couple of occasions, and after getting badly whipped, they were no longer much of a threat.

At one o'clock the small convoy took off, with the usual pair of armed men and women in the cab and at least two arm guards in the truck bed of each. When they got to Leroy's convenience store, one truck continued up the road a ways to watch for traffic and another lagged behind in the other direction. As soon as the first two trucks filled their tanks, they replaced the two guard trucks, which then joined the line to fill up. Everyone not involved in the actual driving and filling process were formed in a perimeter around the area looking out for any hostile threats.

When all the tanks and gas containers were filled the convoy headed back to Sea Breezes, and the guard trucks that were out on watch fell into line. It was easy this time. Car owners would be able to partially refill their tanks from the gas cans.

Leroy walked over to Josh after everyone had left and said, "Josh, my shop's gas tanks are about empty. They weren't full when the Collapse hit and the two times we've gone out have pretty much drained them. I measured and there's less than a half a foot left in each of the gas tanks. The next time we go, we need to take only diesel trucks or cars, and there are only a few of those around here."

Josh nodded, and said, "Well, Leroy, it's not like we're going to be taking any long trips. Things would have to be pretty desperate to even think about leaving the island and heading into the mess that is Port Monroe now. I was thinking that if things got really bad for us, maybe we could join up with the Army guys at the airport. But I don't think taking in refugees is part of their mission, so I sincerely doubt it would do us any good, even if we didn't get ambushed along the way. They've got to take care of their own, and I'll bet the troops are on low rations themselves."

"Yeah, that's what I think too. But you know we've got to go out farther to scavenge, and really the only thing left is individual homes. And that will be tricky."

Chapter 15

A week went by, but they hadn't even seen another aircraft anywhere in the area. Then one morning they saw six more planes of various types and sizes approaching the airport and landing. An hour or so later, several Blackhawk helicopters circled over the city and also landed at the airport. People ran out of their houses to look, including Rich and Sophia. Rich smiled and said, "Well, that settles that question. These new guys are here to stay awhile. I guess what with so many of our larger city ports being taken out by the dirty bombs, Port Monroe is looking pretty good to the government now."

Sophia said, "Probably, but we still need to get some more food or some people are going to start getting sick and die soon. We've already had two more cases of Cholera in small children since Julia's announcement. We can hope all we want but that doesn't put food in our bellies."

"I know, Hon. Josh and I've been planning another scavenging trip, only this time out to the houses in the area that aren't part of one of the three developed communities. We think there are at least 80 or 90 individual homes that were built early on, and as gruesome as it may be, some of the owners never came back, some have died, and some have been killed.

"We may find a few homes with some food still in them in the few areas we haven't visited yet. And don't worry, we'll make sure that we don't take anything from homes that are still obviously occupied."

Sophia looked at Rich and said, "That's good, Rich. I'd like to go along on the next run too. If we do run into people alive, it would be best if a woman were to do the initial approach to talk with them."

Rich thought a minute and replied, "That's a good idea, Sophia, but you have guard duty this evening. Why don't you stay behind for this one and rest up? I'll make sure that we have a couple of women along with us when we go. Some people already know about us going out again tomorrow, but I'll put the word out at tomorrow's meeting."

Sophia really couldn't argue with him so she just said, "OK."

He kissed her on the forehead, put his arm around her, and they walked back inside to give Tasha the few scraps of leftovers they had saved for her from their meager lunch. It's a good thing Huskies like fish.

Chapter 16

Jacob Holmes and Ana Serrano liked each other, but their marriage, or more accurately their cohabitation, was more one of convenience than true love. Unlike Julia and Bill, they hadn't bothered going though even a rudimentary wedding ceremony, and had come together mainly for security and physical reasons. Jacob was a young man in his late twenties, and he had had a girlfriend who lived in Port Monroe, but he very much doubted she had survived. She was a high maintenance woman who panicked if she couldn't find her iPhone. She worked in a law office as a legal assistant, lived in an apartment near her parents, did not enjoy outdoor sports, and would never even think of going camping. She was the proverbial young "snowflake"- an only child whose parents doted on her and never said "no" to her. He sincerely doubted she was tough enough to have survived the first month of the Collapse, much less until now. Plus, her apartment was downtown- not the safest place to be after the Collapse.

On the other hand, Ana was a slender Hispanic woman, pretty, and sexy. But she was among the least prepared in the neighborhood, and one of those who had run out of food first. Jacob was a decent enough guy, he was handy, and she knew he could help care for her. She was thinking of all of that this morning and she smiled to herself and thought, "And the sex isn't bad either."

Jacob came to the breakfast table that morning for something to eat and said, "Anita, I'm going out with Rich on the scavenging party this afternoon. I'll get you something good to eat when we divide up the goods- you don't have any weight you can lose.

"Thanks, Jacob. I've gotta eat something else other than dried fish or I'm gonna' scream." She smiled grimly and said, "Just bring me back a large pizza with all the toppings."

Jacob laughed at that, and said, "I wish. Do you want to come with me?"

"No thanks. I need to work in the community garden this morning since there'll be some folks missing that are going on the scavenging trip. I might as well do what I can to help grow us some more vegetables and fruit. You go ahead, but please be careful."

Jacob got up and kissed her on the cheek, then headed out to Josh's house. He got there just as the pickups were arriving, and went over to talk to some of the other neighbors. Leroy had arrived at the same time, and walked over to talk to Rich and Josh, but before he could say anything, Josh said, "Hey, Leroy. I guess you found someone to replace you at the bridge today."

Leroy answered, "Yeah, I asked Donna and she said she'd like to do something different for a change, so she went out with Malcolm at first light this morning." He turned to Rich, who had a puzzled look on his face. Josh hadn't told him about this switch. Frankly it had slipped his mind. Josh said to Rich, "It's just for one day. Sorry I forgot to mention it, but Leroy has a good idea."

Leroy took the cue and asked, "Rich, can we go by my old house first? When you came and got us out of there we left in such a hurry that I may not have gotten everything out, maybe even some food. I think I had an old case of MRE's in the spare bedroom closet. It's been there about five years, but most of the packaged food is probably still edible. And I'd like to check on some of my neighbor friends to see if they're still around. If not, maybe they might have left some food or something else useful behind."

Rich thought a moment and said, "Good idea, Leroy. You guys were early settlers here on Phelps Island before the developments were built. Maybe the looters missed something in those older homes. We'll head there first, and see what we can find."

By the time three o'clock rolled around, there were six pickups and two cars lined up in front of Josh's house, along with about 40 people hanging around, waiting to go out on the expedition. Everyone wanted to be in on the latest scavenging hunt- just about everyone was looking for food, or had some other needs.

Rich looked around and said, "Josh, there's no way we can control a group this large, and I'd rather not advertise that so many of us are going to be away from Sea Breezes. There may be more watchers out there and I don't want to leave Sea Breezes with so few defenders."

Josh nodded, "Yeah, I agree. We've never had so many people show up before. Let's cull them down to four trucks, four people in each one. We won't need any more than that- there's just not much left out there to be had, and that's enough for security. I'll have the rest go on back home. In fact, I'll stay back too. It's not a good idea to have you, Donna, and me away from Sea Breezes on a risky mission at the same time."

Rich agreed saying, "Thanks, Josh. I was just going to ask you to stay behind for that very reason." He jumped up and stood on the back of one of the pickups and announced their decision. He then picked four drivers and 12 shooters, omitting Fred Carlucci, whom he didn't trust in many ways, especially as someone who would be expected to have his back in a gunfight. There were groans in the crowd and Fred, obviously frustrated, hollered out, "Screw that! We all know that those who go out get the best food for themselves. I'm going, goddam it!"

Rich walked up to the man and looked him in the eye and said, "Fred. No, you're not. I tell everyone who goes out with us every time that if I see someone stealing for themselves they'll go before Donna and risk get expelled from the community. We divide everything we get equally for all residents as soon as we get back. That's always been the deal, and that's the deal this time."

Fred, a coward at heart, backed down, turned away, spit on the ground and said "Shit." Then he stomped off back to his house. Rich turned back to the group of men and women they had selected and said, "Let's mount up, folks."

Chapter 17

Rich told Leroy to take his truck and lead the convoy out, and he'd follow behind in the next pickup. One of the men from the last pickup in line got out and jumped inside one of the cars that were always blocking the Sea Breezes' entrance (keys for all were hidden behind the passenger visor). He backed the car back the car up to open the barrier, then after the convoy had passed, pulled the car back in place and hopped onto the back of the last pickup. The convoy headed out to Beach Parkway, and turned right towards the beach, then turned south towards Leroy's place. They didn't pass a single soul along the way. Leroy stopped his truck and pulled over after the turnoff on the street he had lived as soon as all the pickups had made the turn. He got out and shouted, "Rich! Tell everyone to look alive. Remember, I got attacked in my home here back in February."

Rich made sure the word got passed back and the folks in the back of the pickups perked up with their rifles and shotguns raised, scanning outwards as they slowly drove on another block to Leroy's old home.

Leroy lived in a modest middle class area- not an organized community- and no HOA rules to hassle with. Most of the homes were of brick and concrete blocks, nicely kept up by proud owners.

But now it looked like a war zone. Lawns had been taken over by weeds, and trash strewn around everywhere. There were bullet holes in the front doors, and windows had been shot out of many of the homes. On some houses, front doors had been ripped open. There was no one was in sight.

When Leroy got to his house he got out and looked up and down his street. He cupped his hands around his mouth and hollered, "Hello in the houses! This is Leroy Ivory, coming back to my home. Anyone out there?"

All he heard was silence.... The trees swayed in the breeze, and a plastic bag blew down the street. Everything looked abandoned and forlorn. Leroy had locked his door on the way out when he left, and he pulled the keys out of his pocket and opened the bullet-ridden door again. He stepped inside, and was surprised that it was just as he had left it. If anyone had come in through the shattered windows from the attack, it didn't look like they spent much time inside. He went straight to the spare bedroom and looked in the closet. There, under some spare blankets and sheets were not one but two cases of MRE's. He smiled, shook his head, and mumbled to himself, "Damn. I'm gettin' old. My memory's sure not what it used to be."

Not that in this case he was disappointed though. He bent down and picked up both MRE cases, then carried them out and tossed them into the bed of his pickup. That's when he remembered something else. The attacks had come on the 18th of February. He had bought Althea a present for her birthday on the 22nd, four days later, but had never had the chance to give it to her.

He went back into his house and went into the small third bedroom that had served as his and Althea's office. He opened the closet, reached under some file folders and pulled out a box of Whitman's Sampler chocolates.

Like many people, Althea was a true chocoholic. So was he, for that matter, and when he bought the candy he knew he would share the box of chocolates with her. But then, he thought, "Well, these are no longer Althea's or mine. If it weren't for the Sea Breezes community, I'd have never recovered them." He took the box out to the pickup also, and put it in the front seat of the cab.

While Leroy was looking for other items he might have forgotten, other folks had spread out to the other nearby houses and were looking through each one for anything useful. Before anyone went inside a house, a guard was placed in the front and back, and then the house was hailed from the front door. No one had responded from any of the houses.

In some of the houses, the scavenging party found dead bodies- some shot, some emaciated, others obvious suicides. But in most of them they found at least something useful. In one, a half full can of coffee; two piles of newspapers in a garage that could be cut up and used as toilet paper (the stack of National Geographic magazines were left in place- the pages were too slick to use); some spices; a container of flour with weevils in them- no problem- cooked weevils could be eaten too; some batteries; a couple of plastic bottles of bleach. They'd even found some cans of food hidden away for a rainy day that the occupants never lived to eat. Not exactly the mother lode, but already enough to justify the trip.

Leroy and two of his companions moved on down the street while the others searched the houses behind him. After the security precautions had been taken, he knocked on doors and hailed the houses, but no one answered.

He had hoped to find one of his neighbors still alive. Then he thought of a good friend who lived four houses down and he set off in that direction to check on him. But halfway there he realized he'd gone too far without his two men, and turned around to go back and get them. Just when he did, two shots rang out.

Leroy's back arched with the impact of the bullet. Several of the Sea Breezes guards came running and were shot at from the house 20 yards down the street where the road curved to the left. One of Leroy's men took a round in his thigh. Fortunately, it was an in-and-out flesh wound, but he went down hard onto the pavement. They could see that there were at least two men shooting from the front windows of the house.

The Sea Breezes men and women near Leroy who could see what was going on returned fire, keeping the shooters' heads down, with them only able to fire off the occasionally badly aimed round. Rich and the team from his pickup were in the house across from Leroy's and heard the shots. Rich turned to his men and yelled, "Follow me!" He led the three men out the back door, behind the house they had been searching. After listening a moment for the direction the gunshots were coming from, he quickly gathered them and told them what they were going to try to do.

The four men took off through the back yards until they came to the back of the house across the street from where the shots had come from. When all were caught up to him he put them in a line behind him and said, "Sounds like two shooters. I'm going to step around the corner of the house and when I can see the first window, I'll start firing.

"You guys roll out behind me and get on line. The two of us on the right will fire at the window on the right, the other two at the window on the left. Don't stop advancing and firing towards the house until I call cease fire. He looked each man in the eyes and saw heads nod. He peeked around the corner again and said, "Let's go." Rich stepped out just as one of the shooters popped up and started firing down the street. Rich shot at him and kept firing as he walked towards the front of the house. The others came on line beside him, everyone firing as fast as they could. After no more than 30 seconds of unrelenting fire, Rich yelled out, "Cease fire! Cease fire!"

They hit the ground, changed magazines and waited, but no sound came from the house. Rich grabbed the man next to him, a big, solidly built young man by the name of Greg Gibson who was armed with a semi-auto shotgun, and said, "Let's go- front door. You others watch the windows and the sides of the house in case someone comes around from the back." The two moved slowly in a crouch towards the front door, rifles up by their cheeks, looking over their sights, eyes and barrels moving back and forth between the windowsills and the front door.

When they got to the front porch, Rich yelled inside, "Put down your weapons or you'll be shot!" There was no answer, so Rich set his rifle down on the front steps and drew his Bersa 9 mm semi-auto pistol. He crawled back near the door and whispered to Greg that on his signal, he should kick the door in. He motioned that he would go in low and pointed to the left, and that Greg should go in after him high and scanning to the right.

Greg nodded his head that he understood. Rich looked at Greg and pointed at the door. Greg raised his big right leg and kicked the door in with his boot, knocking it completely off its hinges.

After a slight pause to make sure no one was shooting at them, they both entered the house. Rich went in first through the door, scanning to the left. Greg followed with his shotgun up and looking right. Both scoped out the entire living room area, but neither saw any movement. There were no shots fired.

They saw two men and one woman inside. One of the men near the window on the left lay on his back with a bullet hole in his forehead, eyes open with a look of surprise on his face. The other man had taken a round in his throat and was gagging, still alive, sitting up on the floor. His carotid or jugular was partially severed and he was breathing in some blood. The man looked up at Josh, and mumbled, "What the...." He coughed up a clot of blood, and before he could finish the sentence, he slumped over on his side and passed out. They knew the man was no threat and that he had only seconds left to live.

There was a woman lying down flat on the floor to the left of the window. Her wrists and feet were tied tightly with nylon cord. Somehow she appeared to be unhurt by the fusillade of bullets. She was whimpering and crazy with fear and had obviously been beaten and abused, but at least she hadn't taken a bullet. As she started to rise, Rich lifted his hand up and patted downwards to indicate that she should stay down. He hustled to the back door to see if anyone was trying to get away.

He looked through the window in the back door and didn't see anyone outside, so he opened the door and stepped out onto the back porch. A big man who had been hiding with his back flat up against the back wall of the house stepped forward and swung his rifle by the barrel at Rich.

The blow caught Rich hard on his left shoulder when he instinctively raised his arm as he saw the movement out of the corner of his eye. The butt of the rifle only grazed the side of his head. The blow dazed him a little, but if it had caught him in the face, he would have been down for the count. As it was, the blow briefly numbed his left shoulder and arm, and the jolt made him drop his pistol.

The big man dropped his rifle, stepped behind Rich, locked an arm around his neck and began choking him. Rich struggled a few moments, but with his left arm still numb, he couldn't break the hold with just his right hand. He was still dazed and struggling for breath and knew he would pass out soon, unable to speak or breathe.

Rich knew he had to act quickly. He bent his legs and pushed his body back with all of his strength, slamming the man hard against the brick wall. He heard the man exhale with a "whoosh" and his grip loosened slightly from the impact. Rich raked the choking arm deeply with his fingernails, and the man pulled it away just enough for Rich to catch his breath. He bent his head down, and bit down hard, causing the man to scream and pull his arm away.

Rich pulled the bitten arm down and to his right with his right hand, pivoting his own body around so that he was now behind his attacker. He pulled the assailant's arm up behind his back, then slung his weakened left arm around the man's neck in the same type of choke hold that had been used on him. But Rich had been trained in Ranger school on a hand-to-hand combat technique called "the rear strangle takedown." He slammed his right knee into the man's back as hard as he could, then let both of their bodies slam to the ground as he maintained the choke hold. They hit the ground hard, as their combined weight doubled the force of the impact, and the man's neck broke as soon as he hit the ground. There was no need for Rich to continue applying his choke hold, but he did anyway just to make sure.

Greg came out the back door with his pistol raised to see what the commotion was all about, just as Rich was picking himself off the ground. Rich was breathing hard and said, "The girl. Go see if she's OK."

Greg nodded and went back into the house. He slowly approached the agitated woman and untied the cord that was binding her wrists. The woman immediately started screaming and scrambled back into a corner, babbling incoherently and screaming, "No! No!"

Rich staggered into the room and looked at the panicked woman. He held both of his palms out to try to quiet her and ease her fears. She stared at him with an expression of panic, so he didn't try to approach her again. Instead he backed off and told Greg to go get Rebecca, his wife, to come and care for her.

Chapter 18

After a minute or two, a petite young redhead dressed in jeans and a T-shirt came to the door and knocked cautiously as she peeked inside. Rich motioned for her to enter so she walked in and said, "Rich, I'm Rebecca Gibson. My husband said you needed my help."

Rich was still breathing heavily but managed to say, "Good, Rebecca, thanks." He brought her up to speed on what had happened. "There are three scumbags here who kept this woman tied up and probably abused her. She's pretty messed up, as you can imagine. Greg untied her wrists, but she won't let us near her. I think it would be better if you talked to her and calmed her down. Tell her we'll take her to an aid station and get her treatment for her injuries. When she's calmed down, bring her out to your truck and let her sit in the cab with you while you drive. We'll be heading back as soon as we can get loaded up. I think we've had enough for one day."

Rebecca looked over at the young woman and whispered to Rich, "Got It. Why don't you step outside and let me talk to her." It wasn't a question, so he headed for the front door.

Although Rich wasn't aware of it, while all of this was going on, Leroy lay on the sidewalk on his back, shot through the spine and liver, bleeding out.

His last thought was, "Looks like I'm not going to be eatin' any of those chocolates with Althea."

Leroy grimaced in a final burst of pain, exhaled a deep sigh, and died with that last thought.

Rich jumped off the porch, grabbed his rifle, looked down the street and saw several men crouched around a prone figure. As he approached the group he realized that the prone man was Leroy, and started running. When he got there he saw a pool of blood spreading around his body, and looked down into the lifeless eyes of his friend. "Oh my God, Leroy!" He looked up at the men standing around him for confirmation and one of the men shook his head. "Rich, by the time I got to him he was already gone. There wasn't anything we could do."

Tears came into Rich's eyes, and he stood up and said, "Ahh, shit." After a long pause, Rich wiped the tears from his eyes and said, "OK, help me pick him up and we'll lay him down in the bed of my pickup. We'll leave as soon as everyone gets back and loads up whatever supplies they found. When we get back to Sea Breezes, Jacob and I'll take Leroy back to Althea and break the news."

He and Jacob carried Leroy to the pickup bed and Rich looked back towards the shooters' house and saw Rebecca with her arm around the frightened young woman, walking down the porch steps. Her husband, Greg, had already pulled their pickup up to the curb. Rebecca got the sobbing woman into the cab, then went around to the driver's side, got in and drove the pickup back to where Rich stood. Rich walked up to her window and said, "Rebecca, when we get back, take her directly back to Julia and have her look her over. We'll drive slowly, and when we get back to Sea Breezes, keep going on over to the aid station." He turned around and hollered, "Everyone, back in the trucks." Then he went over to his pickup and slid into the driver's seat.

He took a moment with his head down and eyes closed, thinking how close he had come to being killed. It had been damn stupid of him to walk out that back door without considering there might be someone behind it, and if the guy hadn't run out of ammo, he'd be dead.

He turned around, waiting for the other vehicles to fall in line. Once everyone was in line, he fired up the motor, eased off the brakes and led the convoy home.

Chapter 19

When the convoy got back to Josh's house, Rebecca kept on driving towards Julia's. Josh heard the trucks arrive and came out of the house. He noticed right off that everyone was glum instead of the usual smiles and joking after they had come back from a scavenging mission. Rich got out of his truck and walked up to Josh. As he was approaching, Josh noticed the blood on Rich's chin, the red welt around his neck, and his disheveled clothes. "Rich, what the hell happened?"

Rich looked at Josh with tears in his eyes said, "Josh, we we lost Leroy. His body is in the bed of the pickup I drove." He then went on to give a brief summary of what had happened. "My stupidity almost got me killed too, Josh."

Josh shook his head and said, "Damn, Rich. Leroy! I can't believe it. I thought that old Marine would outlive us all. Shit."

He wiped the tears from his eyes, put his hand on his brother-in-law's shoulder and said, "Rich, don't be too hard on yourself. You got out of a tough situation and all the bad guys are dead. Listen, why don't you go inside and clean up a bit? You look like hell. I'll take the pickup with Leroy and go tell Althea."

Rich said, "OK, Josh, but wait a minute for me and we'll both go. She'll want to know everything that happened, and I can tell her."

"OK. While you wash up, I'll go break the news to Carmen and ask her to come too. She can stay with Althea for a while." They went back inside Josh's house and in a few minutes they both came out, Carmen crying and shaking her head.

Carmen looked at Rich and said, "Damn it, Rich. How much more tragedy can we all take?"

Rich looked at her with sympathy in his eyes, shook his head and said, "I don't know Carmen. As much as we have to I guess." He paused and then said. "C'mon, let's take Leroy back to his wife."

Josh nodded in agreement, turned around and looked over at his son and said, "Sean, unload everything from the trucks and put it all in our living room. Stay here and when we get back, we'll break everything down into equal shares so we can hand it out at tomorrow morning's meeting.

Josh walked over to the pickup bed and looked down at Leroy's body. He picked up his cold hand and said, "Semper Fi, Leroy." That brought more tears to his eyes, so he wiped his hand across his face and climbed into the pickup bed. Carmen was sitting on the passenger side of the cab and Rich got in and drove off towards Althea's house.

It was a little after five o'clock and Althea had just returned from the community gardens, her back aching from stooping down and watering plants by hand. The knock on the door came and she opened it. She saw Rich, Josh, and Carmen, and the looks on their somber faces. She put her hand to her mouth, her head moving from side to side and said, "No. Oh, no, not Leroy. Please, not Leroy."

Carmen came in and wrapped Althea in her arms and said, "I'm so sorry, Althea. Let's go sit down." They all walked into the living room and Carmen and Althea sat on the couch, with Rich and Josh sitting in chairs across from them.

Althea said, "Just tell me what happened. How did my husband get killed?" Rich told her an abbreviated version of what had happened and then handed her the box of Whitman's Sampler. There was a card scotch taped to it. "Here, Althea. He had just gotten this from your house."

Althea looked at the box, then peeled off the card, opened it and read it silently. It said:

"My dearest Althea,

Happy birthday to my favorite gal. You're still as beautiful as the day we met, and I'll love you forever.

All my love, Leroy

P.S. Can I have the coconut creams?"

Althea dropped the card into her lap, leaned into Carmen and sobbed. The box of candy slid to the floor. The two men watched, helpless, with lumps in their throats.

After a few minutes of uncomfortable silence, Althea said, "I want to see him." Rich nodded and led her out to the pickup. Althea climbed into the pickup bed, looked at the body of her husband, knelt down and softly kissed his cheek. "I love you, Leroy. I truly do."

Chapter 20

Twenty minutes earlier, Rebecca had led a trembling young woman, into the aid station. Greg had run to the door ahead of them and called for Julia. He quickly explained to Julia what had happened and finished just as Rebecca walked in the door with the young woman.

Julia called to her stepdaughter, Nichole, to come help. Together Rebecca and Julia stood on each side of the woman, took her into a bedroom and helped her lie down on one of the two single beds. The young woman looked around the room, her eyes wide with apprehension, and suddenly relief swept over her face. She realized she was with people who would help and not hurt her, and she calmed down.

Julia pulled up a chair next to the head of the bed and held the young woman's hand. "Hi. I'm Julia and I'm a nurse. What's your name?"

The young woman wiped a strand of blond hair back from her face and said, "My name is Charlotte. They killed my parents and took me...." She faltered and started sobbing again, her shoulders heaving.

"That's OK, Charlotte, you don't have to tell me everything now. Just tell me, where do you hurt? What can I do to help?"

Charlotte looked up at her and said, "They raped me. Like animals, they took turns with me whenever they wanted, then kept me tied up except to go to the bathroom. Those bastards treated me like I was a play toy, a dog, a whore."

Julia looked at her with compassion and said, "OK, I understand. Why don't we let you get cleaned up? Go on into the shower and you'll find two buckets of water. I'll bring you some soap, a washrag, and a towel. I'll loan you some of my clean clothes and you can change after you bathe. They'll be a little big on you, but at least they'll be clean. If you need to use the toilet, we've rigged up a chair with a toilet seat and a bucket under it, and you can use that too, if you need to. Would you like that?"

Charlotte nodded her head yes, and got up slowly. Julia led her to the bathroom, got everything ready for her, and shut the door to let her have complete privacy. As she shut the door, she said to Charlotte, "Call me if you need anything. I'll be right across the hall."

Julia's stepdaughter, Nichole had come in and Julia said, "Niki, go get a Xanax tablet from the medicine cabinet and a glass of water. Bring a flashlight too." Nichole took off and was back in a few minutes.

Greg had decided he'd stay behind in the living room, but Rebecca had followed them into the bedroom. She said to Julia, "Would you like for me to stay? Can I do anything to help?"

Julia responded, "Thanks, Rebecca, but I think we're fine. It's probably best if you leave so it doesn't remind her of where she was. Niki and I are new faces in a friendly place, so I think the two of us can handle things for now. Thanks for all your help though."

Rebecca nodded and smiled, "Sure thing. Of course. You know where I live if you need me." Julia smiled and said, "Yes. Thanks." Rebecca left the house with Greg and they walked home.

While Julia was helping Charlotte, the man who was wounded in the leg at the same time Leroy was killed was brought in the front door, hobbling on one leg with the help of Jacob Hanson. Julia had made it clear to Bill that he should stay away from Charlotte for now, so he was in the waiting room when the wounded man came in.

He and Jacob helped the wounded man, whose name was Lou Reston, onto the dining room table and Bill unwrapped the bandage around his lower leg and to look at the wound. Jacob said, "If you don't need me anymore, Bill, I need to head on back to Josh's house to help with the sorting of goods." Bill told him he didn't, so Jacob took off.

The wound was a clean through-and-through on Lou's lower thigh muscle and since he was wearing shorts they didn't have to worry about strands of clothing that could have been shot into the wound. Bill cleaned the blood from around the entrance and exit wounds with soap and water, then carefully dabbed the wounds with hydrogen peroxide. Bill had learned to suture cuts and knew he could sew the entry and exit holes up, but decided to wait for Julia and let her look at the wound before he did anything else. Lou wasn't in any great pain, so they just chatted for a while until Julia came back. Lou joked and said, "Well, I guess I won't be pulling roof guard duty for a few weeks." Bill smiled and said, "I wouldn't count on that, Lou."

Chapter 21

Althea came back into her house after seeing Leroy's body and said she wanted to lie down. She asked Carmen to help steady her as she walked back to the bedroom. She did, and helped Althea into her bed- her and Leroy's bed- and left the room. As she was leaving, Althea asked, "Please have someone wrap him up in a blanket or sheet. We'll need to bury him tomorrow morning."

Carmen nodded, "Of course, Althea. We'll do that right away." She turned to her husband, and said, "Josh, would you go get her a glass of water? Then go over to Julia's and see if she has something we can give her to help her relax. I'll stay here and watch her in case she needs anything. You guys go on, I may be here a while."

Josh went over and put his arms around his wife, and kissed her on the forehead. "OK, I'll be back in a few minutes." He and Rich left the house together, and Rich said, "I'll take the body back to my house, wrap it up, and park the truck in my garage. We'll bury Leroy tomorrow after the morning meeting. After I'm done, I'll meet you back at your place and we can start sorting the goods." Josh said, "OK. I'll see you later."

Rich drove home, parked the truck in his garage, and went inside to find Sophia. He told her about the ambush and Leroy getting killed. Sophia teared up and hugged her husband tightly. "Oh, Rich, I just can't believe this happened to Leroy. It scares me- it could have been you."

Sophia said she would give Rich a hand with wrapping Leroy's body. She went and got a white sheet and went out to the truck. She looked down at Leroy as tears came to her eyes again. Rich carefully rolled the body over while Sophia slid the sheet under him, then he gently let the body roll back down again onto the sheet. They wrapped him up tightly and Sophia used safety pins to secure the sheet.

When they were done, Rich set off for Josh's house, and by the time he arrived he found that after everything had been put in one place, they actually had a pretty good haul, considering. There were the two cases of MRE's that Leroy had found, and about 60 cans of food, along with assorted packages of cereal, most open, and other useful items they had gathered.

Rich looked at everything and realized that this haul was going to be difficult to separate equally. Some may be dying for coffee, some may really want batteries for a flashlight, but most would want food, some desperately. Does a half container of flour equal a half dozen AAA batteries?" How do you divide 24 MRE meals and 40 cans of various types of food, from green beans to pumpkin pie filler among almost 200 people? He sat down and asked that same question of Jacob, hoping for some suggestions.

Jacob said, "Well, Rich, some of our neighbors need food more than others. My Ana is really thin, and so is Carlucci's wife.

"Those kids with Cholera have got to need some extra nourishment too. I think maybe Julia needs to be in on how we distribute what, and to whom. Regardless, no one's going to be happy, and some people will be bitch about it, no matter what we do."

Rich nodded and said, "Good thinking, Jacob. Julia's going to be pretty busy tonight, with that poor girl we brought in and the guy who was shot in the leg. I know she'll want to look in on Althea too. I'll go down and explain our problem. She's going to be a busy woman tonight. But it's times like these that justify why we've exempted her from guard duty. Hell, I remember after the Werewolves' attack, she and Bill went almost two full days without resting, while she treated all of our wounded. I'll go tell her why we need her help on the distribution."

On his way back to Julia's, he met Josh, heading back home. They talked about everything they had to do tomorrow, and Josh agreed that Julia should make some of the calls on who got what kind of food.

When Rich got back to the aid station, Julia had just finished suturing Lou's wounds, so Rich quickly explained why they wanted her advice on food distribution. She said she understood, and that it was a good idea. She would make a list of those who were most in need of nutrition and later on tonight come back and look at the stash of goods at Josh's house, then make up a priority distribution list.

Rich thanked her and apologized for all the work he had dumped on her, but Julia smiled and said, "Don't worry about it, Rich. This is what you pay me the big bucks for. I'll see you at Josh's house early tomorrow morning."

Rich smiled, leaned over and gave her a quick hug, and said, "You're a good woman, Julia." When he got to the street, he turned and waved goodbye to her. She smiled back at him and went inside to wait for Charlotte.

Chapter 22

It was around 7:30 p.m. when Carmen peeked in on Althea again and saw her sitting up, reading the card that had come with the box of candy. Althea looked up at her and said, "I'm going to have one piece, for Leroy. The rest I want to give to the kids in the neighborhood. Lord knows they haven't had much of a childhood these last few months." Carmen smiled at the kindness of the thought, and said, "That's wonderful, Althea. I'll hand a piece to each kid at the distribution tomorrow morning. I'll tell everyone about how it came to be that they get a treat- the whole story."

She had brought in the glass of water and a Xanax, and told her, "Here, take this. Julia sent it over. It'll help you relax and get some sleep."

Althea looked up at Carmen with swollen eyes and nodded. "Good idea. I think I could use some help getting to sleep tonight." She swallowed the Xanax tablet and handed the water back.

"Can I bring you something to eat too?" Althea shook her head, opened the box of candy, looked at the lid to see the diagram of where each type of candy was, and reached in and picked out a piece. "Thanks, Carmen. I think I'll just have one of Leroy's coconut creams."

Carmen smiled and said, "OK. You go ahead and get some rest. I'll see you tomorrow morning. Julia said she'd come look in on you later this evening, but I told her not to wake you up. So don't be surprised if you see someone."

Althea nodded and said, "Carmen, thanks for everything." She sank back into the bed and closed her eyes. Carmen quietly closed the door and headed on back home, the Whitman's Sampler box in her hand.

When she got home, Carmen told Josh about Althea's wishes and he smiled and said, "I'll make sure we do that. I can't imagine anyone complaining about that, but we're going to have a tough time dividing things up for tomorrow. Jacob and I have made piles that are about equal, but I've still got to get Julia's input, and then I'll probably have to rearrange some food. We've got everything in plastic shopping bags, but we didn't have enough for one per person, so I've got them bagged for homes with two, three, and four family members. That was the only way we could think of to make sure to get at least some food for each family.

"Jacob had the idea to split up the MRE's so everyone will get something to eat. We also held back eight complete MRE's for anyone Julia feels really needs some extra nutrition. MRE's may not be the most palatable food in the inventory but they're high calorie and loaded with vitamins. We also held out a big bottle of 300 multivitamin and mineral tablets. Julia will have some idea on how to distribute those also. I think that's all we can do for now. When Julia gets here tomorrow morning we can finalize everything."

Carmen sighed and said, "That sounds good, Josh. I can't think of anything more fair than letting people pick up their own bag, contents unknown. I think we've done all we can today. I'll fix us all something to eat, then let's go to bed. I'm emotionally and physically exhausted after everything that's happened today."

Josh said, "OK, 'chica'. I'll give you a hand. Do I need to start a fire?"

"Not tonight, Josh. It's crackers and canned jelly, and an orange split four ways for supper."

Chapter 23

Sophia woke up and looked out the bedroom window at the gray haze and light drizzle. Her first thought after shaking the sleep from her head was "I hope this ends before we have to bury Leroy. Digging a hole in the rain isn't going to be any fun." She looked over at Rich, with his four-day growth of beard, and smiled. No need to waste soap, water and blades for daily shaving any more. The beard does make him look older though, what with the gray coming through. She shook him awake and when he opened his eyes she bent over and gave him a quick kiss on the lips. "Morning, sunshine."

"Ahh, shi.... What time is it?"

"It's 6:25, and it's starting to drizzle outside."

"Great. Nothing like holding an outdoors meeting to hand out food in the rain. At least they tied the food and stuff up into plastic bags. Speaking of food, let's go get something to eat."

"Let's not," replied Sophia. We should wait and see what we get in the way of food this morning and then we can eat something if there's enough.

"Josh, I hate literally not knowing where our next meal is coming from, or when we'll get it. With the little we have left, and the little we'll get, we might have enough to eat something twice a day for the rest of the week."

"Sophia, let's not argue about this again. You need to eat more and you know it. We'll get some more food today. The fishermen and women are going out again tomorrow, so we should get some fish day after tomorrow."

"But, Rich, even going out every other day, they're not bringing back much, and they're having to go out farther and stay out longer each time. All they have are a couple of canoes, and one rowboat we found during our scavenging trips. All of them are on a QRF team too, and they conduct reaction drills around every part of Sea Breezes once a week on top of that. They put in twelve hour days and we can't ask them to do that more than every other day."

"OK, Hon. There are still some dry dandelion leaves left so I'll go fire up some tea. But we will have a decent lunch today, and a supper. After we finish the tea let's head down to Josh's and help him and Carmen move the goodie bags over to the picnic area." Rich kissed his wife again, threw on a T-shirt and a pair of shorts, and left to light up the BBQ grill to boil some water.

While the water was heating up, Rich called Josh on the walkie-talkie and asked what time they should arrive to lend a hand. Josh said to come about 8:30 since all they needed to do was move the bags up to the two tables under the pavilion at the picnic area. Josh reminded him that Julia would be there a little after 8 with a list of folks who needed extra nutrition.

Rich and Sophia arrived right at 8:30 as Julia was finishing up separating the eight MRE's into seven piles of MRE packets, one entree for each of the three adults she had designated to get the extra rations, and one for each of the four children recovering from Cholera. All the MRE toilet paper would go to the two families with the four children that had come down with Cholera. Those kids didn't need the chewing gum, matches, or plastic spoons, so she slipped those into some of the other bags to be distributed. They put the extra entree into the bag of the only family of six in the community.

None of the kids got any of the spicy entrees, like Chili Con Carne or Chicken Curry either. Instead, they got milder entrees with mostly beef, like Braised Beef in Gravy and Beef Tortellini. Julia said she'd take care of handing out the vitamins at the meeting.

Rich asked Julia how Charlotte and Althea were doing. Julia replied, "Charlotte is really doing well, considering. Unless she ends up pregnant or with some STD, I think she'll be OK, eventually. She seems like a pretty good kid, and she's not emaciated or anything, so her parents must have had a good supply of food stashed away before they were killed. I guess she'd have to be tough to have survived all that she went through. It turns out that she was caught in their home when the three thugs broke in and killed her parents. She'd only been with the men a couple of weeks when we found her, but that was enough to mess her up psychologically. She's only 19 years old, and otherwise in pretty good overall physical health.

"I talked to Althea on the way over here. She's really a tough woman. She volunteered to let Charlotte stay with her in her home. She said Charlotte would be good company for her now that Leroy was gone. That was very nice of her and, frankly, I think it will be good for both of them."

After Julia's update, they all got together and decided that Rich would lead off the meeting to let everyone know what had gone on the day before during the scavenging trip, and how the distribution of food and goods would work. He'd be followed by Carmen and Julia. Carmen would tell everyone about the candy for the kids, and Julia would explain the extra food going to those who needed it. Josh would go last with some changes to the duty rosters because of losing two men.

Everyone picked up three or four plastic bags in each hand and started taking them over to the pavilion. By the time nine o'clock had rolled around, everything was in place and, as was the routine on days after scavenging trips, there was at least one person at the meeting representing each household present. No household would be able to try to sneak extra rations. They used an old list of residents to check off each house, and Josh made sure the list was updated every time they lost someone.

Fortunately, it had stopped sprinkling a few minutes before the meeting was to begin. Rich was about to step up on a table to get everyone's attention when he looked over and saw Charlotte and Althea slowly walking up towards the lake together. He and others who had noticed the latecomers looked at them solemnly, and waited patiently for them to arrive. Once they had gotten to the outer edge of the crowd of residents, he stepped up and began the meeting.

Rich quickly explained the tragic events from the scavenging trip, adding that they had rescued a young woman, Charlotte, who was now part of their community. He gave no details of the circumstances of her captivity. He was pleased to hear several people shout out a welcome for her. Charlotte had tears running down her face, and even managed a smile for everyone.

Rich pressed on. He also told them that immediately following the meeting, they would be going out to the burial ground they had established in a corner of Phase II. There would be a brief ceremony honoring Leroy before the burial. All were welcome to come and he asked several men by name to bring shovels. Althea remained stoic at this pronouncement; she was determined not to cry.

Rich then told everyone they would pick up their share of the scavenged goods as usual, but that this time they would choose from piles of bags according to family size instead of getting one bag per person. He explained why, and to his surprise, no one complained. He then said, "This afternoon at five o'clock, we'll have another Sea Breezes bazaar. That way if you get something you don't want or need, you can try to find someone to trade with for what you do need." That got a little cheer also.

"OK, any questions?" He paused, but apparently everyone wanted to get on with the food distribution so he said. "If not, then Carmen needs to tell the kids something."

Carmen stepped up and began, "I'd like to announce a little treat for the children." She then explained that Althea wanted to give her 24-oz. box of Whitman's candy that Leroy had bought for her birthday to the small children. She also mentioned that Althea had taken only one piece for herself, so that left 59 pieces. "We'll do this by age groups, but any child who's old enough and likes to eat chocolate candy, please come see me after the meeting. We'll first take kids 10 years old and younger and then add another year in age until the candy is gone. As soon as the meeting is over, kids, come find me over at the pavilion."

Julia stepped up onto the table as Carmen got down, and several children started running over right away until Julia hollered, "Wait, kids! Not yet. Wait until the end of the meeting. I'll say when."

She smiled and shook her head at their eagerness. She thought, "My, how things have changed, when kids can get so excited about getting one small piece of chocolate."

Julia continued. "I've also designated several people who in my opinion as a nurse, need extra nutrition. When the parents of the four children recovering from Cholera come to pick up their share of the distribution, see me afterwards for some extra food for the kids. They're MRE entrees and very nutritious. I've also designated three adults who also need some extra food." She read out their names: "Ana Serrano, Sheryl Carlucci, and Sophia Cantrell." Sophia looked like she had been poked with a stick and stood up, starting to say she didn't need any extra food. But before she could speak, Julia cut her short. "No arguing. You will each get an extra entree, and you are to eat it yourselves. We don't have one person we can afford to lose due to weakness from malnutrition, not with all the work and guard duty that needs to be done.

"Also, every head of household, after you pick up your bags from Josh, I'll be handing you some multivitamin and mineral tablets. Every person in your family should take one with his or her next meal. It's not much, but it's something, and every little bit helps. The parents of the four kids recovering from Cholera will get three extra tablets for each of the kids to take with meals once a day."

When Julia had finished, Josh stood up and made some changes to the guard and QRF team rosters. He also announced that Jacob Hanson would take Leroy's place watching the bridge every day for any traffic coming and going.

After he stepped down, and while he was still thinking about it, he walked away from the crowd, pulled out his walkie-talkie and made a quick radio check with Jacob.

The bridge was only two miles away, but the transmission sometimes broke up and had to be repeated. So far they were always able to talk to each other, even if it took some repetition. One good thing about the scavenging trip yesterday was they found a stash of batteries, and all of them had several months left before their expiration date. He wondered how long after a battery's expiration date it would still be of use, but he had no idea. He thought. "I've got a lot more important things to worry about than battery life."

Everything went fine on all of the distributions, and Sophia and each of the other two women accepted the extra MRE entree with a combination of resignation and gratitude. Rich wisely said nothing to her about it, but he'd make sure she'd eat at least half of the entree at lunch. Almost all the residents looked into their bag as soon as they got it, and you could see that most were disappointed at first glance. Well, at least they'd have a chance to do some bartering and swapping at the bazaar.

Chapter 24

Only 29 people showed up for Leroy's ceremony after the meeting. It was a low turnout, but death was no stranger to the community since the Collapse. They had already lost 37 souls due to attacks, sickness, and suicides, so one more wasn't a big deal to most of the residents, their thoughts elsewhere. Most were busy going through their bags of goodies, wondering how much and what kind of food and other items they had gotten.

The sky had cleared up earlier, and that made digging the grave easier. Three men and two women had pitched in to help dig a hole five feet deep and six feet long, and two men laid Leroy's corpse into the hole. Donna was there, and she said a few words about Leroy, then led them all in the 23rd Psalm. Althea didn't speak at the ceremony, but she was the first to throw a handful of dirt into the grave. Those close to her heard her whisper, "I love you, Leroy."

One of the homeowners was something of a carpenter, and it fell to him to make a wooden headstone with the name of the individual buried, and the date of death. For the Christians he painted a cross, and for the Jews he painted a Star of David. Some had neither.

Those who showed up for the burial didn't stick around after the brief ceremony. They wanted to get home to see what they had gotten in their goodie bags, and maybe eat something right away.

On the way home from the burial, Josh walked with Rich and talked to him about the desperate food situation. Josh said, "Got any ideas, Rich?"

"I can think of a few options, all of them bad. We can make another scavenging trip soon, but we'll have to go back to the area near Leroy's old home, and we may run into more scumbags, and end up in another shooting match. We could also try to drive into town and try to make contact with the Army force, but we'd probably have to fight our way there, and since we can't communicate with them, there's no way to make sure that they wouldn't think we're hostile and shoot at us. We've both heard a lot of gunfire over there in the past few weeks.

"Or, we could try to find a motorboat so our fishermen could go out further than they can now with just their paddles and oars. No sense in trying to send out hunting parties anymore. No one has seen so much as a squirrel or a dog in weeks. That's why we keep Tasha on a leash whenever we go outside and we never let her off unless we, or someone we trust, has eyes are on her all the time."

Josh said, "Yeah, none of those are very attractive, and we can't make the few crops we have grow any faster. I sure wish to hell we knew what's going on with the government. In the weekly updates we get on Donna's Ham radio, it seems like they're making progress in the big cities and around the military bases, but I'd love to know what plans they have for the troops they sent into Port Monroe. That's our only hope for some sort of food relief in the foreseeable future."

"I agree. So, of all those options, let's try one more scavenging trip. We'll wait a couple of days, then hit the other homes in and around where Leroy used to live. Other than Sunset Beach and Pelican's Landing, that's the only area we haven't scavenged yet. I don't want to pick a gunfight with either of the gangs in those two communities, not even the Werewolves. The fishermen come back tomorrow evening, so let's see what they bring us that we can hand out at the next morning's meeting. But we probably need to go ahead and plan for another scavenging trip day after tomorrow."

Josh said, "Sounds like a plan to me. I'll see you at the bazaar at 5."

"OK, Josh, see you then. Hang in there."

"I will. Make sure you get Sophia to eat her MRE meal."

Rich just nodded and headed up the sidewalk to his house.

Chapter 25

When Rich walked in, Sophia had, for lack of a better word, "brunch" ready. She had some coffee they'd gotten in their bag from the distribution, enough to make a small pot. She had opened a can of tomato soup for Rich, and the MRE entree for herself. She looked at Rich and said, "I'm sorry, Rich. I know I need to eat more, and I won't embarrass you again for being so thin. I'll eat my half of whatever we have for each meal, and I'll finish everything on my plate. I've just got to trust that we'll find some food somehow. I know I can't allow myself to get weak and still be alert and effective."

Rich reached over and laid his hand on hers and said, "Sophia, you could never embarrass me. But thanks, I'm glad you understand." He could have said more, but he knew to quit when he was ahead. They both started eating, slowly, savoring every bite, and chatting in general about the community.

Sophia said, "I made the coffee, so there's enough for each of us now and for you to have a cup before you go on roof guard duty tonight. It'll help you stay alert. I know you've had a tough couple of days."

"No more than you have, Sophia- or all the rest of us for that matter. I don't know of anyone that's slacking off. I'm especially glad that Sheryl Carlucci got some extra food too though. She was looking very weak and I know she works as hard as she can on the community garden.

"Josh and I were talking about the food situation and we've concluded that the only thing we can do is go out on another scavenging trip to those houses we were at yesterday. We'll tighten up security procedures so that no one goes near a house without first putting some guards out on the street a couple of houses ahead also. God, we're still learning too many things the hard way."

"Well, don't blame yourself, Rich. You and Josh have done a great job in getting security organized for Sea Breezes; and, well, shit's going to happen sometimes, no matter how well you plan."

They both continued eating in silence for a while. When they finished, Sophia said, "That was great, Rich. I feel better already. Let's clean up here and go to bed."

Rich said, "OK, but I'm not really sleepy. And I don't want to to sleep through the bazaar."

Sophia looked at him with a seductive grin and said, "Who said anything about sleeping?"

Sophia led Rich into the bedroom and they undressed, pausing only for a passionate kiss as they embraced before they lay down on the bed beside each other. They caressed each other, hands roaming and touching, softly murmuring sighs. Sophia rolled on top of her husband and made slow love to him as she stared deeply into his eyes. It had been a while.

A half hour later, Rich did fall asleep. Sophia was also drowsy but she looked at her watch and decided she should get up and feed Tasha. Their poor Husky was skin and bones, and they had gotten a can of Vienna sausages in the distribution. She fed Tasha one of the sausages and part of a cracker. She did that off and on while she cleaned up the house, making sure Tasha's system could handle the food. Tasha had a cast iron stomach though, and she had no bad reaction at all.

Sophia remembered back on that first day they picked her up from the pound how Rich had first gained her trust by offering her some warmed up pieces of a hot dog. It seemed like a lifetime ago.

At four o'clock she woke Rich and told him she had fed Tasha. Rich smiled, as she didn't know that Rich had already slipped her an MRE cracker while they were eating. He put on his shorts and T-shirt, and went out to play with Tasha in the back yard. She was feeling the strength from being fed and she wanted to frolic, so he spent five minutes throwing a tennis ball for her to fetch. She never seemed to get tired of the game of fetching and having him wrestle the ball from her as she growled ferociously. He decided he'd take her to the bazaar so she could play with the kids. Tasha was the only dog left alive in Sea Breezes.

He and Sophia walked up to the lake area with Tasha on a leash. They had a few items, like a hunting knife, and some lightweight clothing, to take to swap just in case they could do so for any kind of food. There were no takers.

The bazaar was well attended, and no one created any trouble. If there was any food swapped for goods, Rich didn't see it. Some people traded one type of food for another, and some items for different things, but no one was giving up any food. They left for home after wandering around and talking to people for about 45 minutes.

The fishermen weren't back yet, but they knew the routine. Clean their catch, save the entrails for bait, wrap up the fish in newspapers, and distribute them next morning to the next houses on the list. There hadn't ever been enough to give everyone a fish, so they had developed a system for distributing each catch, based on the old amended homeowners list. Tomorrow, the next 21 homes on the list would get a fish, the larger fish going to the larger families. Day after tomorrow, the next homes on the roster would each get a fish each from the catch. It wasn't a perfect system, but it worked.

Was there cheating among the fishermen? Maybe, but Rich and Josh had long ago decided not to waste a lot of time trying to check on each catch. If the men and women who went out and spent 12 hours on the waves of the gulf took an extra fish for themselves, they couldn't blame them.

At a quarter of eight, Rich grabbed his DPMS Puma 5.56 mm rifle and his Bersa Thunder Pro 9 mm pistol, walked down to the corner guard post, and climbed the ladder on the side of the house. The guard left his rifle with Rich, as per procedure, but Rich wanted his own rifle- it was zeroed in perfectly for 100 yards.

Chapter 26

Rich returned home from guard duty at 6:30 and made himself some coffee with the leftover grounds from the day before. Sophia was still asleep, but he left her a cup on the edge of the BBQ grill, then lay down on the couch for a while. Sophia woke him at 8:45 and reminded him to go up to the nine o'clock meeting.

Nothing much went on at the meeting, and there were only 60 or so men, women and children. The fish had already been distributed to those on the list, and of course some hopefuls were disappointed they didn't make the cut due to the small catch. Julia gave out the remaining vitamin pills from the original bottle of 300 tablets to those who had bothered to come. She thought, "Well, at least these people cared enough to show up." The few tablets she had left over she would save for the Cholera kids or anyone else needing some extra vitamins and minerals. She wasn't sure how much of a difference they would make, but it couldn't hurt. The four kids had recovered from the disease, and so far there had been no other cases. Julia had scared everyone into taking strict precautions with their water.

At the meeting, Rich announced that there would be another scavenging hunt, and asked everyone to get the word out, because they would be leaving right after the next morning's meeting.

It would be organized the same as last time, four trucks, 16 people, only Josh would be leading this one, and Rich would be staying behind. They would head out at 10.

As the meeting was close to breaking up, Josh received a call on the walkie-talkie.

"Josh, this is Malcolm, come in."

Josh fumbled for his radio on his hip, and pressed to talk, "This is Josh, Malcolm, what's up?

"Josh, we just... (garbled, static)... and they... (garbled)."

"Malcolm, you're breaking up. Say again, slowly."

"OK. We just saw three vehicles and ... (static)... motorcycles heading... (static) the bridge... (garbled)."

" Malcolm I understand you saw some vehicles leaving the island, correct?"

"Yes. I say again, yes, over."

"Is it all clear? All clear?"

"Yes. Yes."

"I'll be there in five minutes. Be there in five minutes, over."

"OK. OK."

Josh clipped the radio back onto his belt and yelled, "Rich! Hey, Rich, come here!"

Rich heard, turned around, and saw Josh waving his arms and ran over to him. "What is it Josh? Everything OK?"

"Yes, I think so. From what I can tell, it sounds like the Werewolves have decided to leave the island. We need to grab a couple of shooters and go talk to Malcolm and Jacob."

"Greg and Rebecca are right here and they bought their pistols. Grab a couple of rifles for us and let's take your truck and go find out what's going on. I'll go tell everyone the scavenging trip is postponed until further notice."

It only took a few minutes to get everyone loaded up in Josh's pickup, and they roared out of Sea Breezes, everyone in the truck keeping a watchful eye on the road for any stragglers or other traffic. They got to the bridge in less than five minutes, pulled around back behind the strip mall, and parked.

Rich jumped out of the pickup bed and jogged into the old cafe through the back door. The three others followed right behind him. When they all had entered he said, "Jacob, what did you guys see, exactly?"

Jacob was excited and spoke rapidly. "Rich, we saw one car, three pickups, and four motorcycles, heading off the island into Port Monroe. It was the Werewolves, or what's left of them, and the pickups were loaded with boxes and bags, probably food, heading our way. I pulled Malcolm back from the window and we watched them all speed across. They must have had a destination in mind, because they were still speeding as far as we could see them. I guess they wanted to make sure they got by anyone who might be right on the other side of the bridge. We heard some gunfire shortly after they were out of sight, but not like a real battle or anything."

Josh paused a second and said, "My God, that's big news. That means that Sunset Beach is probably abandoned. Who knows what they left behind, but we need to go find out, and now, in case the Zulus saw them leave. Maybe they didn't, but we can't take that chance."

Rich nodded and said, "OK, you guys stay on guard here, and call us if you see anything else coming or going." He turned to the others and said, "Let's head back. We need to put together a scouting party, ASAP. We'll do it like the last time we went out to Sunset Beach when we negotiated the prisoner exchange with the Werewolves after their attack on Sea Breezes. We'll take six trucks and 24 shooters. Let's go!"

The four got back to Sea Breezes as fast as Rich could drive, and on arrival began spreading the word. There were still a few people hanging around the lake area wondering what was going on. Josh enlisted them to help get the word out. The message was, "All hands on deck, everyone armed and ready." Some who showed up would be left behind in case of an attack.

Forty minutes later, most of the adults had showed up at the lake with their weapons. The first 24 who were there with rifles or shotguns were assigned to ride out in the trucks going to Sunset Beach. The rest were told to reinforce the roof guards and to assemble whatever remained of the QRF teams and send them out near the four corners of the subdivision. Those left over would guard the entrance road. No one knew what to expect of the Zulus, or for that matter if any Werewolves were left behind to send Sea Breezes a few parting shots. It took another 20 minutes to get the scouting party formed up.

Rich jumped up on a pickup bed and said, "Listen, those of you who went with us last time to Sunset Beach, we'll be doing the same thing this time. How many of you were there then?" About a third of the crowd raised their hands.

"OK, you vets make sure there are two of you on each truck so you can show the newbies what to do. Basically, we'll stop a couple of hundred yards from the gated entrance, everyone but the drivers will get out of the trucks and advance on line with weapons out. Those riding with me will be walking on the entrance road and the rest of you will be on my flanks with weapons searching for bad guys. Don't fire unless someone fires on us, or you see someone getting ready to fire on us. Got it?"

There were rumbles of "Yeah," and, "Got it." Rich said, "Alright, let's mount up and head out."

Chapter 27

The convoy stopped just when the gated community came into sight. The shooters deployed, and the drivers idled forward at walking speed. Everyone was scanning to the front, sides and rear for trouble. As Josh and his team walked towards the entrance gate, the first thing they noted was that it was wide open.

Rich turned to his team and said, "Gate's open and I don't see any guards." He brought his hands to his mouth to make a megaphone and yelled, "Hello in Sunset Beach! Anyone home?"

There was no answer. Everything was quiet and still, and no one saw any movement. Rich then hollered to the group, "Stop where you are, get down, and cover us." He said to his team, "Spread out and we'll walk up slowly up to the gate. Weapons ready and scanning. Follow me."

Rich arrived at the gate first. He checked the guardhouse and no one was there. He looked around and all he saw were houses with windows shot out, trash everywhere, and a burned out car. He motioned for his team to follow him and they all walked through the gate and spread out, looking everywhere. Nothing moved. Rich hollered back, "Bring up the vehicles, everyone come on in, and spread out."

Sunset Beach was the wealthiest community in or around Port Monroe. It consisted of 44 individual homes and two four-story condos, each floor having four to six apartments. It was a gated community with a six-foot high steel fence around it.

There was only one road in the community and all the homes were large McMansions. The road ended in a circle, so about half the homes were on the beach and the other half were across the street from the beach or on the circle. There was also a small marina in between the two condo buildings.

The scouting party started moving down the street and then a lone man walked out of the fourth house on the left with his hands raised. Rich shouted, "Stop where you are. Keep your hands in the air." He turned to one of his men and said, "Go frisk him for weapons." The man did and escorted the stranger back towards Rich.

Rich looked closely at the stranger. He looked like the walking dead he was so exhausted. He started to ask, "What's your n...." but stopped. Then his eyes lit up in recognition, and he said, "I'll be damn. You're Dr. Rajan- from the hospital. You gave us some medical supplies and equipment, a few days after the Collapse."

Dr. Rajan squinted his eyes and said, "Yes, you're the man who came with the nurse. Julia was her name. I'm sorry, but I don't remember yours."

"I'm Rich Cantrell. But what the hell are you doing here?"

"I live here." Dr. Rajan said. "In this house." He indicated over his shoulder the house he had just walked out from.

Rich said, "How did you survive? "Why did they let you live? Are there any others?"

Dr. Rajan held up his hands and said. "So many questions! Best that you let me tell you the story. You are safe here. There is no one else left alive in Sunset Beach except for my wife and my two young sons. Everyone else is dead or gone, except for two wounded men they left behind who are too bad off and couldn't be moved. They will die soon, I'm sure."

Rich started to interrupt with another question but Dr. Rajan held up his hand and said, "Please, let me continue. When the Werewolves came, they arrived in the early morning. They started at the closest houses to the gate, kicking in doors and shooting people. Some of my neighbors down the street came out to see what was going on, but the gang fired on them and they quickly ran back inside their houses. I watched from an upstairs window.

"After slaughtering everyone in the first three houses before the condos, their leader, a big bald man they called 'Stalin' yelled out for the men to stop firing. They set up a quick perimeter and attacked the two condo buildings, killing anyone on the ground floor or who came out of their apartments. When they got to the roofs of the condos, Stalin stationed men with rifles where they could see the entire community.

"When they got to my house, instead of shooting they pulled their guns, kicked in my door and yelled inside, "Come out and you won't get hurt." I had locked my family in our bedroom, so I left my wife and children upstairs and came down with my hands raised. I identified myself, and told them I had a wife and two children upstairs, and that we were unarmed. Stalin looked at me, thought for a few seconds, and said, 'A doctor, huh? We might be able to use a doctor, so if you do what I say, maybe I'll let you live.'"

"Stalin continued, 'Here's what you're going to do. You and your wife are going to go now and knock on everyone's door on down the road. They'll recognize you, so you figure out how to get them to open the door and talk to you. You tell them what you've seen, and that they have until noon to come out to the gate and they'll be let go. No vehicles, no weapons, just what they can carry. They'll be allowed to leave on foot or bike, but they won't be returning. Anyone still in their homes after noon will be shot. I'll hold your kids here to make sure you come back. You got all that?'

"I couldn't believe what I was hearing and didn't answer fast enough. Stalin stepped up to me, slapped me hard and screamed 'Got that, Nigger?' I answered yes, and decided it was best not to correct him and tell him I'm Indian. There was nothing else I could do, so I called for my wife, and she came downstairs. I told her what we had to do and she looked at me in horror. I told her, 'We have to do this or they will kill us and the boys.' There were tears in her eyes, but she nodded her head. There was nothing we could do but yell up to the boys to stay in their rooms. Stalin sent a man upstairs to watch them. We left, and started walking down the street together, knocking on doors.

"Some people wouldn't open their doors. I don't know if they were not at home or scared. It took us two hours but we finally relayed Stalin's message to everyone who opened their door to listen to us.

"Some people said hell no. Some said that they were armed and would fight. I told them that there were at least 40 men and women with guns that I saw, and probably more. I said that resisting or not complying would mean their death.

"By the time we finished it was about eleven o'clock, and families had already started moving towards the gate, carrying plastic bags and rolling suitcases. A few came on bicycles and were allowed to leave with them. By 12:15 there were no other people in the streets. Stalin gave the order to check out each house.

"His men went house to house, kicking in each door and searching upstairs and down, and outside. I heard a few screams and gunshots over the next few hours. One of the Werewolves was shot in the shoulder by a homeowner.

"Two men helped him into my house, and that was how it became a medical clinic. I had plenty of medical supplies since I always kept some at home; and, on the last day I worked in the hospital after the Collapse, I took a car full of more supplies, equipment, and instruments with me when I left the hospital, so I could treat the members of my community. I had not envisioned being taken hostage and all of my neighbors being killed."

There were tears in Dr. Rajan's eyes by the time he finished. Everyone listening was just staring at him with their mouths open, not able to imagine the horror of what went on that day in the community. Dr. Rajan caught his breath, got control of himself and continued.

"Over time I had a lot of work to do. I heard they were going to attack the Sea Breezes community." Rich interrupted and said, "That's where we're from." Dr. Rajan nodded and went on.

"I'm not surprised. You shot them up very badly, twice. Only a few came back from their second encounter with you- the ambush.

"With those left behind to guard Sunset Beach, there were only 13 men and women left in total, and six children of various ages. I counted, and when they left here there were only 17, leaving the two seriously wounded behind. They took as much food as they could carry. I heard them talking about going back to Port Monroe and leaving the city. I never heard where they were heading, but with the military planes landing, they knew that they would be trapped on the island if they didn't leave soon."

Exhausted, Dr. Rajan said, "Forgive me, but if you don't have any more questions, I need to get back to my house and tell my family that we're safe for now."

Rich said, "I do have one question, doctor. What's the food situation here?"

"Ah, yes. You are undoubtedly low on food. How on earth did you survive? Never mind, you can tell me later. To answer your question, they took food from the homes and brought it to the condos, where they had set up their headquarters. They seemed to be careful with food and rationed it out, but I think with all the casualties they took, they have quite a bit left. They bought me food for my patients and a little for my family every day. If there is any food storage it would be somewhere in one of the condos. They occupied some of the homes too, so there may have been some left in those houses. You should look."

"Don't worry, doc, we will. By the way, what's your first name, if I may ask?"

"Yes, of course. My name is Ahmad. My wife's name is Aisha." He paused a moment and asked, "What will become of us, Rich?"

Rich had already decided. "Ahmad, we have a couple of vacant houses in Sea Breezes. Some residents never came home after the Collapse, and others were killed or have died since. We're a well-organized community and we've survived many attacks, large and small. You're welcome to come live with us, if you like. We certainly could use a doctor to help out Julia."

Dr. Rajan thought for only a few seconds, "Thank you, Rich. I will talk to Aisha, but I'm sure she will agree to take you up on your kind offer. We have been prisoners here for a long time and we don't want to stay here alone because we have no way of defending ourselves. I don't think we could live here anymore, or ever again; she will be glad to put this place, and the nightmare we've endured here for the past five months, behind us."

Chapter 28

Rich looked at his watch and saw it was already 12:45. He called Josh over and they discussed what to do next and how to go about doing it. They had a lot to accomplish and not much time to get it all done. They absolutely had to get back well before dark so they could get the roof guards in place for the evening shift change. No way was he going to try to do that in the dark. Josh had reminded him that several of those with the scouting party would have duty that evening, including Rich himself.

Dr. Rajan had gone back into his house to talk to his family. Rich and Josh walked over to the marina to check it out, then came back to the trucks. They were deep in conversation for several minutes until they finally came up with a plan for the next six hours. Rich called everyone around him.

"OK, we have to work fast and smart. First, you two" he pointed to a man and a woman on his team, "stay at the gate and watch for anyone coming. If you see a vehicle, fire a warning shot first, and if it keeps coming, shoot to kill. The Zulus could be on their way here for all we know. Also, I need at least four people who know how to drive a motorboat, a big one."

Five men and women raised their hands. "OK, all five of you, go down to the marina and pick a couple of motorboats that you can find keys for. Check everywhere- the boathouse, the glove compartments, or wherever a key may be hidden. Unlock them, untie them, or shoot the cables, or whatever you need to do, and get the two biggest you can start up. We saw a couple of nice cabin cruisers as well as some plain old outboard motor fishing boats. I saw from the top floor of the condo that one of the cabin cruisers had blood all over the deck. I suspect they used that to shuttle the dead bodies out to sea and dump them. Don't be squeamish. If that's one of the ones you can unlock, take it.

Make sure you round up all the gas cans and gas you can find and load them up on the boats you get. While you're looking for gas and keys, search for food and other useful items on all the other boats, and load them up on the two boats you get. Then drive them around to the northeast side of the island and anchor them. Make sure you take a dinghy with you so you can get back to shore. When you get close to where Sea Breezes is, throw out two anchors on each boat, fore and aft, then lock the boats up. Use the dinghy to get everyone to shore, and come on back home. Got it?" Five heads nodded and a few said, "Got it," and took off jogging towards the marina.

"Everyone else, team up two to a house. The doc says everyone has left but be careful anyway, and enter houses weapons up. Look around for food and anything else useful, and stack or pile it in the beds of the trucks. Also look for plastic bags, toilet paper, medicines in bathroom cabinets, and so forth. You know the drill. If you should happen to see anything else really useful, get that too. Use your judgment. Spend enough time in each house, but don't dawdle.

"Drivers, station your trucks at intervals between here and the circle at the end of the street and help load up supplies. I want everyone finished up by 7. All trucks should come back here, then and line up for the trip home. Everyone understand?" There were some mumbles of "Yes and "Yep" and off they went, pairing up as they walked.

Josh gave Rich two men from his truck so they each had three people to check each of the condos. As Rich started to head out to the nearest one, Dr. Rajan came out of his house and said, "Rich, I have talked to my family. We will go with you to Sea Breezes. I have some food to bring with us and I also have the medical supplies that I need to load up. Can you give me a hand?"

Rich said, "Sure, Ahmad." He turned and told the two men with him, "Follow the doc, and help him carry his supplies down to my truck. I'll go and take a look around the first condo. Join up with me over there when you're finished. I'll stay on the ground floor until you arrive."

By a little before seven o'clock, all the trucks had been loaded and were lined up, ready to go. Josh and his team had finished their condo first, so he went up and down the line, quickly checking out what people had found. It was a very good haul, a mixture of mostly canned foods and other supplies. There was no time to take an inventory, but when Rich came down from the first condo, Josh collared him and said, "We got a lot of food and other stuff. We'll offload everything in my living room when we get back and sort it out later. Rich, I believe you'll have to help us do that. I'll find someone to replace you on roof guard duty because I need someone I trust 100% to supervise sorting through our take. No way we can divide it all up tonight, but we can at least let everyone know at the morning meeting that we were successful, and that a distribution will be coming later on in the day."

Rich nodded and said, "OK, Josh. Will do."

Chapter 29

Dr. Rajan and his family came down from their house with the few possessions they could bring with them and loaded them into the back of Rich's pickup. They put the medical supplies in another. He came up to Rich and asked, "What about the two wounded men the Werewolves left behind?"

Rich asked, "What's their status, doc? Any chance at all they'll be able to recover?"

Dr. Rajan replied, "No. None. They are dying slowly because they have wounds that I cannot treat. One was shot in the hip; the other was shot in the shoulder with a shotgun and the bones of the shoulder were broken. Without a surgical team, all I could do was stop the bleeding, repair as much as I could, give them antibiotics, and sew them up. They did all right for a while, and then started to deteriorate. Infection is killing them.

"I was considering giving them a lethal injection after the Werewolves left, but I found I couldn't bring myself to kill. I'm a doctor, Rich, and I just couldn't intentionally take a life."

Rich looked into the eyes of Dr. Rajan and said, "Ahmad, we don't have time to ponder this. Put your wife in the cab of my truck and get into the truck's bed with your children. Distract them, talk to them about anything until we've left Sunset Beach. I'll take care of it."

Rich went over and had a few words with Josh, and Josh, said, "I'll do it, Rich. You lead the convoy out, but drive slowly. I'll be the last truck to leave. I'll wait a minute after you all have left. No one will hear anything. I'll catch up to the convoy in a few minutes."

Rich looked down at his feet, shook his head, and said, "OK. Thanks, Josh. Just remember that they're going to die in agony if we leave them here."

"Yeah, I understand. Doesn't make it any easier though."

Rich nodded, walked over to his truck and yelled out, "Mount up and let's go!" He started the engine, looked over at Aisha, and said, "Mrs. Rajan, things will be much better for you and your family now. I'll take you to your new home as soon as we get back, and you and your family will be safe with us."

Aisha looked back at him with tears in her eyes and said, "Yes, I think so. Thank you, Rich." He started the engine and led the convoy out, heading back to Sea Breezes.

As the convoy cleared the entrance gate, Josh walked into the doctor's house, went up to the master bedroom, and grabbed a pillow off the bed. He went into the bedroom that the two wounded men were in, put the muzzle of his pistol into the pillow and quickly, in succession, shot each man in the head.

Josh gagged, and almost lost his lunch. He thought, "Shit. I never thought I'd have to do something like this." He swallowed hard and went out to his truck. The two men and one woman on his team looked glum. No words were spoken, but one of them patted him on the shoulder as he got into the driver's seat. They all knew he had no choice. Josh got into the driver's seat and eased out of Sunset Beach.

When the convoy got back to Sea Breezes, they were met with dozens of neighbors, all shouting questions. Rich realized he had to take the time to give a short explanation so he hopped back on the bed of his truck and shouted for attention. The crowd quieted down almost immediately, as everyone was eager to hear the news.

Rich kept it short. "We'll give more details at tomorrow morning's meeting, but here it is in a nutshell. We got a good deal of food, and lots of supplies. We also rescued a doctor, Dr. Rajan, and his family." Dr. Rajan raised his hand in acknowledgment from the back of the truck. "They'll be moving into the vacant house where the Elliots used to live. All of you go home and get some rest. At tomorrow's meeting we'll announce a time for a distribution for later that day. We need some time to break it all down. There's a lot of stuff to sort through and divide up, but we'll get it done as fast as we can. I think it's safe to tell you all to go home and eat a decent meal, and unless you have guard duty, get a good night's sleep. I'll see you all tomorrow. And by the way, thanks to the scouting party for all their hard work today. Great job, everyone."

Some applause and a small cheer went up, but everyone was tired from being on alert all day, so the crowd quickly dispersed and headed home. Josh asked for a couple of volunteers to help him unload the booty from the trucks and carry everything into his house. Carmen helped by organizing everything as it came in. Paper products and plastic bags on and around the couch and lounge chair. Food stacked up on and around dining room table and floor. Everything else over by the fireplace.

Rich got back into the truck and drove the Rajan family to their new home. As he opened the door, he stopped and addressed the family, "I want you to know that you are welcomed in our community. We know you are a Muslim family, and we also know you had nothing to do with the terrorist attacks. Everyone knows how hard you worked to save lives after the Collapse until the hospital finally had to close. We consider you a true asset to Sea Breezes."

Ahmad and Aisha both smiled and Ahmad nodded and said, "Thank you Rich. I appreciate what you have done for us, and I promise that we will work hard for the community."

Rich smiled and they all went inside. He briefly showed them around the three-bedroom house and after they had finished the quick tour, Rich helped the family unload their belongings and the food they had brought with them.

When he had finished with the Rajan family, he took Dr. Rajan's medical supplies and instruments over to the aid station. He explained to Julia and Bill Thornton where they had come from, and that Dr. Rajan and his family had moved into the Elliots' former house. Julia was thrilled with both the supplies and the news of Dr. Rajan.

They helped Rich bring everything inside the aid station and put it all in the waiting area. Julia was wide-eyed looking over everything. "My God, what a windfall. All of this stuff: antibiotics, syringes, scalpels, bandages, IV sets. Amazing! And now we have a doctor, a surgeon no less!"

Rich said, "I'm glad you're pleased, Julia. Dr. Rajan may be one of the best finds we've ever had on a scavenging trip." He left them to sort through everything and put the supplies away where they belonged. When he had finished there he returned to Koenigs' house.

While Rich was gone, Josh and Carmen had looked over everything and agreed that it was as good a haul as they had ever gotten on a scavenging trip. They started the detailed sorting of everything, by type, in each location. Plastic bags, here, newspapers there. Canned food on the floor, boxed food, flour and sugar canisters on the table, and so forth, so that they could get a general idea of the total quantities of each category that they would have to divide up tomorrow among all the residents.

Rich came back after about an hour and pitched in. A half hour later they declared they had done as much as they could until there were more hands on deck to start bagging everything, and Rich left for home. They agreed to meet back at Josh's house at 8:30 the next morning. They were all tired, and emotionally wired from the long day's events, and needed a good night's rest.

Chapter 30

About the time that Rich and the Koenigs had decided to call it a day, the five Sea Breezes "sailors" were dropping anchor on the east side of Phelps Island, less than half a mile from the back gate of Sea Breezes. Among the five were Jacob Hanson- he was a handy man to have around anything mechanical- and Fred Carlucci, who actually had been a good addition to the crew because he had some experience with boats. They had commandeered a medium sized, four-bed cabin cruiser, the one that the Werewolves had used to transport bodies out to the depths of the gulf to dump them.

As it turned out, it was the only boat with an inboard motor that they could find the keys to, and that one was easy- the keys were still in the ignition. But they had to spend almost an hour dumping buckets of water across the back deck to scrub off the dried blood from the decks.

They couldn't find keys for the three other larger cabin cruisers, but they did get a small fishing boat with a pull-start outboard. The six sailboats in the marina were of little use to them, so they left them after they had combed them for useful items.

They had been able to siphon enough gas to fill the cabin cruiser from the other boats in the marina, and they had gathered up all of the portable gas cans they could find and filled them. They stored these inside the cabin cruiser.

They also found some food stored aboard the various boats, as well as some fishing gear that would come in handy. The Sea Breezes fishermen only had small fishing rods meant for lake, river and shore fishing, but they had found two rods and gear for deep-sea fishing among the marina's boats.

The five men and women had motored both boats to the north, and around the tip of the pear-shaped island, and then headed south a short distance and dropped anchor not far from where the near empty expanse of Phase II was. They used the small inflatable boat on the cabin cruiser to shuttle back to the island, and walked back towards the back gate, waving at the guards so they would be recognized. They were all back in Sea Breezes just before dark.

Since Rich's house was not far from the back gate, Jacob stopped off and let Rich know that they had returned and briefly told them what they had accomplished. Rich was pleased and told Jacob so. "Thanks, Jacob. Tomorrow it would be helpful if you and Fred would take the fishermen and women out to the boats, show them around, and teach them how to operate both. The outboard boat should be pretty easy to operate, but they'll probably need some instruction and practice on running and navigating the cabin cruiser. The last thing we need is for the crew to run the boat onto a shoal or get lost out there. You guys can meet up after the morning meeting tomorrow."

Jacob agreed, said good night, and headed back to Ana's house. He was pleased, once again, at the thought of now having someone to go home to.

Chapter 31

Rich and Sophia arrived at Josh and Carmen's house at 8:30 the next morning. After looking through all of the loot they had gotten the previous day, they decided they needed about two hours to sort everything, and they had enough goods and plastic bags this time to use one bag per person in each household.

They had over 200 cans of food, ranging from soups to vegetables to fruit, and dozens of boxes of cereal and mixes. They even found a few boxes of powdered milk that they set aside to give to families with very young children. Along with the food were an assortment of batteries, tools, paper products (mostly old newspapers) and soaps of various kinds. There were also several boxes and bags of contents from people's medicine chests, and these were set aside for Julia, and now for Dr. Rajan also. Sophia said, "I'm glad we're going to have to get used to saying Dr. Rajan's name along with Julia's. Actually, I guess it's Dr. Rajan's aid station now. At any rate, it's great to have a doctor in the community."

The four adults walked together over to the picnic area and already there was a large crowd. Rich was pleased to see that Dr. Rajan had brought his whole family along. He went up to the doctor and said, "Dr. Rajan...." but the doctor interrupted him.

"Rich, please, it's Ahmad."

Rich smiled and said, "Yes, thanks, Ahmad. I'm glad to see you brought your family along." He turned to Aisha and her children and said, "Welcome, again, to you all. Thank you for coming."

Aisha said, "Several neighbors came by to introduce themselves, and they all talked about the daily meetings, and said it was especially important to come today to find out about the food distribution."

Rich said, "Well, we're not ready to hand out the bags of goods yet, but I'm going to announce a distribution for noon today, as well as a bazaar at 5 this afternoon, so people can swap things. Your whole family should come to both events so you can see how we operate." Dr. Rajan smiled and said that they would.

At a little after 9, Rich stood up and started off by wishing everyone a happy Fourth of July. Some had actually forgotten what day it was. Rich continued, "We'll have reason to celebrate today as we got a pretty good haul of food yesterday." He gave a brief account of yesterday's events, and then introduced the Rajan family. After that he discussed the noon distribution, along with the usual procedures. He asked for two volunteers to help bag and carry the loot over to the covered pavilion after the meeting.

Josh got up and made some changes to the guard roster; Julia announced that they had another suspected case of Cholera, and this time it was one of the elderly residents. She reminded everyone again about purifying all their water for drinking, tooth brushing, and dishwashing, and to wash their hands often, especially after going to the bathroom. "I know some of you are using soap sparingly in order to conserve it, but it's essential to use a little every time you wash your hands. Besides, we have quite a bit of different types of soap to hand out today to replenish your supplies."

Donna Fleer, who had the only HAM radio receiver in the community, got up and reported that the president had spoken to the nation from Camp David again, and that the U.S. was making progress in many areas and hoped to have nation-wide radio coverage by the end of next month. Once that net was established, everyone would be able to listen for at least an hour a day for news, updates, and even local weather in some areas, but probably not in the Port Monroe area.

Fred Carlucci asked all of the fishermen and women to meet him at the back gate at one o'clock so he could show them the boats and how to operate them. Everyone was excited at the prospect of having the new motor boats and getting more seafood every other day.

The meeting broke up and everyone headed home. They could hardly wait until noon rolled around.

The distribution went well. People were excited and most were pleased. Those that weren't would have a chance to swap or barter for what they wanted at the afternoon bazaar.

The bazaar also went off without a hitch. A lot of people wore colorful red, white and blue clothing and many brought American flags with them to celebrate the fourth. Rich was on rooftop guard duty but Sophia brought Tasha along to play with the children. The atmosphere at the bazaar was almost festive. Everyone had some food in their stomachs, and that lifted their spirits.

Chapter 32

Martin Goldman was the head of the fishing squad, a position he naturally acquired because he was an avid fisherman. He had no formal title but the other men and women just started calling him "Captain," a tongue in cheek reference to the two canoes and one rowboat fishing "fleet" he "commanded." Martin took the ribbing good-naturedly.

Martin had been a supervisor at the Port Monroe oil refinery, and it was lucky that he had taken a week off from work when the attacks began. He knew how to organize and direct people and with his fishing experience was a perfect fit for the job.

Martin was also one of the men who initially opposed Rich and Josh in setting up a guard force. He had even gotten into an argument with Josh and had taken a swing at him. But when the residents voted to establish a guard force, he reluctantly pulled his share of rooftop guard duty. In fact, he stopped the first major attack on Sea Breezes when he opened fire in the dark of one early morning on a group of Zulus who thought they could easily stroll into the community and loot a few houses. His shooting killed several of the attackers and alerted the community of the assault. After that, no one, including Martin, objected to the necessity of the security forces.

With the boats and additional gear from Sunset Beach, Martin decided they could go out every day now that they didn't have to only paddle or row. With the addition of the motorboats, they could go further out into the gulf where fish would be more plentiful, and larger. They would also use two different teams, one for odd days, headed by Martin, and the other for even days, headed by Fred, so he had to find some more volunteers. They were exempt from the boring roof guard duty, so he suspected there would be plenty who wanted to join his now larger "fleet."

On their first day out they caught 23 fish, some over a foot long. The large fish could be split in half, so they could probably serve the next 30-40 people in the homes on the list. Since they left a fish for family, covering all the houses would take about 85 fish. If they could do that well every day, and they estimated they'd be able to go out five days out of the week, the other two being down days because of weather or maintenance, each home would get a least one fish to eat once a week.

Of course, when they started using small nets, they occasionally caught other seafood too, such as shrimp, but they calculated all sea creatures other than fish into roughly equal proportions by weight. One small fish once a week per house wasn't a sustainable diet for the community, but it sure would help.

One of the big problems of the community was the boring and hot (now that it was full blown summertime) roof guard duty. Some had rigged up overhead ponchos or blankets to keep the sun off, but it still got hot, even with the breezes that came in off the gulf. After suffering from several deadly attacks, however, no one believed the guards should be eliminated. It was a tough job, but it had to be done. There were five roof guard positions, one at each corner of Sea Breezes and one at the entrance. So for three shifts a day, fifteen people were needed. And there were two sets of roof guards that rotated every other week.

The bridge observation team was now being rotated also. Although it was easy duty sitting in the closed cafe by the bridge, it was even more boring than being a roof guard. No one questioned the need for that additional duty either, especially since it was the bridge observation team's alert that had led to the very successful scavenging trip out to Sunset Beach after the Werewolves left the island.

The community garden was now managed by Althea Ivory. She had taken Charlotte- the woman they had rescued from the three scumbags- with her to the garden and she had turned out to be a good worker. The garden was getting bigger, and it was getting plenty of sunshine and rain, but it yielded only so many vegetables. Things were better overall now, with the increase in the fish supply, but the total food supply still was not sustainable in the long run. In the back of everyone's mind was, "How are we going to survive once the island is completely picked over and the scavenging trips have to stop?"

Chapter 33

One early morning in late July, Louise Goldman, Marty's wife, was looking at her watch. It was 6:25 and her replacement hadn't shown up yet. Was it a screw-up in the roster or did someone oversleep? She knew the latter was more likely. Hell, she had overslept once herself, as had many others. Then she heard a strange noise that caused her head to jerk up. "What the hell is that?" She thought, "Is that a freakin' garbage truck? Did the last scavenging party also pick up a garbage truck to use and nobody told me about it?"

She saw the truck was heading right for the entrance so she stood up to wave it down. Then she heard shots being fired from the southwest corner of the community, and thought, "What is that shooting about?" She turned back towards the truck and it looked to her like it was going to ram into the cars blocking the entranceway. Then she realized that was exactly what the driver was going to do and raised her rifle to fire. Before she could pull the trigger her mind registered some louder shots being fired from somewhere across the street and simultaneously she felt a sledgehammer hit her in the center of her chest. She sensed herself falling backwards and instinctively put an arm out to keep her from falling off the roof, but by the time her hand hit the shingles, everything had gone black.

Josh had seen Sean off earlier to go on rooftop guard duty, and he was getting ready to go out and check on the roof guards himself, something he did almost every morning, since the night shift was the most frequent shift to have difficulty in the turnover. Too often people slept in and didn't relieve the guards on time. When that happened, people got mad, so he had long ago decided it was best to find any problems early and get them resolved quickly in order to maintain peace and harmony among the guard force.

As he was heading out to his truck, he heard gunshots from the southwest corner. "Oh, shit." He thought. "That's where Sean is." He was relieved somewhat when he heard some answering shots from Sean's booming shotgun.

Josh reached down to his waist and pulled out the walkie-talkie on his belt. He called Sean- his was Post #2- but got no response Then he heard more fire coming from the entranceway, and he tried to call that position, which was Post #1. He got no response there either.

The entranceway roof guard position was just around the corner from his house, so he grabbed his rifle and ran towards the entrance. As the guard position came into sight, he saw a woman's body roll off the roof and hit the ground. At the same time a big trash truck came barreling into the entrance, easily knocking aside the two blocking cars where they joined front to front. More shots rang out as two pickup trucks, loaded with a total of four Zulus, two in the back of each, came after the garbage truck with men and women firing from both the back and passenger sides. The vehicles initially followed the garbage truck moving slowly down the road towards the lake, shooting into houses. When they reached the circle around the lake, the two pickups peeled off onto a feeder street and drove deeper into Sea Breezes. The rate of fire increased at both of Sea Breezes' southern corners also.

Josh jumped behind an array of mailboxes and fired at the pickups, hitting at least one man. There didn't appear to be any more vehicles coming so he figured that the two pickups and garbage truck were all there was to the raiding party, and there was probably a vehicle at each of the southern corners with shooters firing at the roof guards.

He ran back to his house and made sure Carmen and the kids were safe. Carmen was crouched down on the living room floor with their 14-year-old daughter, Anita. He told Anita to stay where she was and barked to Carmen, "Hurry and go get your rifle. Then come back here and keep watch by the window in case they come back this way."

He covered the street from the window until Carmen got back, then he took off back towards the picnic area and playground. He got there just in time to see two children on the slide in the playground gunned down from a pickup that went roaring by. He brought his rifle up and returned fire, but the pickup was moving fast and he was winded from the run, so his shots missed. He kept on going to the picnic area and when he got there he turned over a picnic table and got behind it, watching where the entrance road met the circle around the lake. Unless the pickups went out the back way, through the garden and the fields beyond, they would have to come back towards him as they left, and he'd be ready for them.

Within seconds, nearly everyone in the community realized what was going on. They didn't know who, or exactly where, but they knew they were being attacked in broad daylight by someone. Those with weapons ran and got them, and the QRF team members began moving towards their designated rallying points. But this was something they hadn't planned for- a raid with vehicles in broad daylight- and confusion reigned.

Deeper into Sea Breezes, a woman was shot in the back as she ran towards her QRF team's rallying point by a gunman in a fast-moving pickup. In turn, the other two members of the QRF team laid down a hail of bullets that took out the driver, and the pickup rolled to a stop in the middle of the street. This happened near the back gate as Sophia came running out of her house and saw what was happening on her street. She began firing her shotgun at the men in the back of the truck, hitting at least one of them. Then the second pickup came roaring around the corner firing at her back. Sophia was hit and went down in her front yard between the two vehicles. The second pickup did a hard U-turn and the two survivors of the first pickup came running past Sophia to their escape vehicle. As one of them was passing Sophia, he turned around and raised his pistol to shoot her lying on the ground when all of a sudden a black blur hit him in the chest and he felt vice-like jaws latch on to his throat.

In fights, Huskies instinctively go for the throat. Several months ago, during the Werewolves' assault, Tasha had grabbed hold of a man's arm, the closest target within reach, only to get shot in the hindquarters. But it at least served as a distraction from the man firing at Rich, and Rich was able to kill him as he tried to fight off Tasha. Maybe Tasha had processed this result back in her primitive brain, and this time decided to follow her instincts.

Regardless, the Zulu went down with his throat ripped apart, and seeing this, the second pickup accelerated away with the one man they had rescued, firing back over their shoulders at Tasha, Sophia, and the two members of the QRF team. No one was hit, as the adrenaline of the shooters combined with the swaying of the truck as it peeled away destroyed any accuracy the Zulu gunmen might have had.

As the garbage truck and the one remaining pickup approached Sea Breezes circle around the lake and turned on the entrance road to escape, Josh started firing from his position behind the picnic table. He hit two men in the pickup, one of whom fell over the side and flopped on the pavement. The garbage truck and the pickup managed to escape despite a hail of gunfire from Josh and one of the other residents.

Shortly after the two trucks left Sea Breezes, the firing at the other two corners stopped, and a car at each corner pulled out and headed for the road back to Beach Parkway. In order to get there they had to pass by the Sea Breezes entrance, but with the roof guard down, no one was watching and they simply turned the corner and made their escape without anyone firing a shot at them.

The residents of Sea Breezes were stunned at the silence that followed the attackers' departure, and slowly came walking out of their houses, hiding places and cover, with guns raised, warily looking around for more intruders. But they had all left.

Four minutes after the shooting stopped, Josh got a call on his walkie-talkie. "Josh, this is Greg at Post #6, come in." Josh's mind was blank, then he remembered. It was Greg Gibson at the bridge observation post. He fumbled the radio and dropped it as the adrenaline release from the stress wound down and he started shaking. He finally got hold of the radio and answered, "This is Josh, what's up?"

"This is Greg. We heard a lot of shooting coming from up your way and then a bunch of vehicles came roaring from your direction and crossed the bridge. They were moving so fast we only got a rough count. It looked like a big garbage truck, along with four pickups and three cars, about 25 or 30 people, maybe more, including some children. What the hell happened up there?"

Josh responded, "We were hit by the Zulus. From what you're telling me it looks like a quick raid on us on their way off the island, probably to take revenge on their losses to us on two occasions. Stay there and let us know if any of them returns from Port Monroe, or if anyone else follows them, but it looks like they've all hauled ass off the island to take their chances in the city."

"Shit. Anyone hurt?"

"Yeah, several. I don't know how many yet. Listen, stand by and we'll talk when you come off shift. I've got to see how bad we were hit."

"Roger, Josh. I'll say a prayer for you guys."

Chapter 34

Rich was on roof guard duty in the northwest corner. He was able to see some of what was going on, enough to realize they were under attack from men in pickup trucks, but he only got a few shots off at the moving vehicles off in the distance as they came and went in between houses. His instinct was to get off the roof and run check on Sophia, but he knew he had stay on watch, in case there was another attack from the north. He didn't like waiting, and he was worried sick the longer he was up there without hearing from anyone. Finally he saw Rebecca Gibson, carrying her rifle, coming down the street toward him. She was returning home to get her car after responding to her QRF team's rallying point they had established for attacks on the neighborhood. He called her name and motioned her to come over and talk to him.

"Rebecca, what do you know about the attack we just had? I couldn't see much of anything from here."

"Rich, I didn't see everything from my position but I know we were attacked by some Zulus in pickup trucks, firing into houses and at anyone outside they could see. I heard we stopped one of the pickups and killed the Zulus in it though. I also heard we took some casualties, but I don't know any of the specifics.

"Would you do me a big favor? Would you go see if Sophia is all right? I'm worried about her."

"Sure thing, Rich. Give me a few minutes." She turned and jogged off towards the Cantrell's house, which was only two blocks away.

Rich sat down looking over the edge of the roof out towards the empty fields of Phase II, and worried. But there was nothing else he could do until he was relieved.

Meanwhile, Josh was checking on the kids in the playground. One little girl had been shot in the head, and she had died, probably instantly. A little boy, who turned out to be her brother, was hit in the arm, so he called to one of his neighbors nearby to go and get a vehicle to transport him to the aid station. He remained with the boy, applying pressure on the wounds to his arm with a piece of cloth torn off of the child's T-shirt he had used to wrap the arm.

There was a lot of confusion everywhere in the neighborhood and some people were congregating around the lake area while others went home to check on family. Josh started barking orders, pointing to people, some whose names he remembered, others he didn't. "Kathryn, please do me a favor and go check on Carmen for me. Ask her to go see if Sean is OK, and then have her come tell me." He pointed at a man standing with a pistol hanging from his right arm and said. "Go and check on the northern and the southeast roof guards and come back and tell me if they're all OK. I need to know if they have to be replaced."

Jacob Hanson came up to Josh and asked him if he could do anything to help. Josh answered, "Thanks, Jacob. Go up to the entrance and check and see if the woman who was on roof guard there is alive. I saw her fall off the roof but I don't know how badly she's hurt.

"If she needs help, call me on her walkie-talkie, and I'll get someone to take her to the aid station. If she's dead, go up on the roof and replace her in case the Zulus come back."

Jacob nodded, "Will do."

A car drove up with Julia in the passenger seat. She jumped out and ran over to the little boy next to Josh. "I heard two children were shot up here. How's the boy doing?"

"He'll be all right. It looks like a through-and-through without hitting bone, but you'd better take him now to the aid station. The little girl over there is dead."

"Oh, Jesus. Well, help me get him back to the car. We've had several people come in to the aid station already and Dr. Rajan is working on them. Bill is helping him, as is the Koenig girl, Anita. I'm on first responder and ambulance duty."

Josh picked up the boy and waited for Julia to sit down in the back seat, and handed him to her. Rich said, "Julia, would you go up to the entrance first and check and see if the woman who was on guard there is alive? If she is you can pick her up too. It'll save you a trip back here.

"OK, Josh, will do." The driver took off towards the entranceway.

Kathryn came back and told Josh, "Carmen is OK. She's gone to the southwest corner to check on Sean and make sure he's all right. She'll be back in five or ten minutes."

Josh said, "OK, thanks." Jacob hadn't returned so he assumed the woman who fell off the roof was dead. That meant the entranceway was guarded once again, so he took off running to his pickup so he could drive out to the southwest corner.

When he got there he saw Carmen sitting on the grass with Sean's head in her lap, crying. He thought to himself, "Oh my God! Sean!" Sean had taken a bullet to his chest and Carmen had taken off her T-shirt and was pressing it over the wound and checking his pulse. It was faint, but it was there.

"Josh, he's alive! We've got to get him to the aid station now!

Josh ran up to his wife and picked Sean up to carry him into the pickup bed. Carmen jumped in first so she could hold Sean's body upright as she kept pressure on the wound. Josh jumped in and headed off towards the aid station. As soon as he arrived he honked his horn several times, and Julia came running out. She helped them get Sean down onto the grass with Carmen holding him in a sitting position. Suddenly, Sean coughed up some blood. He gasped once, and quit breathing. Chest compressions were out of the question. Julia checked his pulse at his throat as it slowed down, then stopped. Sean died before they could do anything else.

Chapter 35

The rest of the day was a confused mess. Josh and Carmen put their son's body back in the pickup bed and drove home. They laid the body out on the sofa in his living room after putting a towel down under his back. They didn't want their daughter to see his body in the back of a pickup truck when she came home.

Sophia had been shot in the lower leg, and her tibia might have been broken. Someone had helped her to the aid station, and Tasha wouldn't leave her side. Rebecca Gibson had gotten the word back to Rich and volunteered to relieve him so he could go check on his wife. Rich thanked her profusely and jogged down towards the aid station.

The fishing party had heard the shots in Sea Breezes from their boats as they were rounding the northern tip of Phelps Island. They had turned around, anchored in their usual place, and made it back to shore. They had come running back with their weapons ready, but by the time they got there, all the shooting was over and the Zulus were long gone.

Rich ran into the aid station and saw Sophia lying on the carpet with a white bandage on her lower leg. "Oh my God, Sophia, are you OK?"

Sophia winced and gave him a crooked smile, "No, Rich, I'm not. Actually, I've been shot in the leg, you big dummy, and it hurts like hell. But I'll be OK. They're treating some of the more seriously wounded, but Dr. Rajan should be seeing me shortly. By the way, when we get home, give Tasha something good to eat- some meat or fish. She probably saved my life."

Sophia explained what had happened and when she was through, Rich bent down and gave Tasha a hug and got a lick in return that left a red smudge on his face from her bloody jowls. "How many people are in here with you, do you know?"

"I got here right after they had brought in a little boy who had been shot in the arm. There were several others here before me with more serious wounds, and others came in later. They're operating on one right now on the dining room table, and the rest of the wounded are distributed in the three bedrooms. I'm not sure of the total, but they all are worse than me, with torso or head wounds. The little boy got his arm bandaged and the holes stitched up and he's resting now, and quiet. I guess they gave him some antibiotics and hydrocodone also. Julia told me he'd be OK. I don't know how many total were hit, or if all the wounded have arrived here yet or not.

"Listen, Rich. Someone told me they heard that Sean Koenig was killed. You'd better go check on Josh and Carmen."

"Oh, Jesus, I hope not. Listen are you sure you'll be OK?"

"Yeah, Rich, I'm all right. Take Tasha with you. She wouldn't leave my side and she doesn't belong in an aid station, but no one wanted to try to separate her from me. Every time someone tried, she'd growl at them and bare her teeth."

Rich looked down at Tasha's and into her big ice blue eyes, and said, "Good girl. Come on." He kissed Sophia and promised to be back soon. Then he took off at a jog with Tasha tagging along towards the Koenigs' house.

When he got there he saw Josh in the garage, unfolding an old sheet. Josh's swollen red eyes told him he didn't need to ask, so all he did was walk up to him, put his hand on his brother-in-law's shoulder and said, "Josh, I am so sorry."

Josh almost broke down but choked back some tears and said, "This sucks, Rich. This isn't fair. Why did my son have to die by those goddam gang-bangers? What the hell is God's reasoning for that?"

Rich knew better than to try to answer, so he said, "Come on, Josh. I'll give you a hand." He guided Josh back inside the house and helped him wrap his son up in a shroud made of the old torn sheet. Carmen watched, along with their daughter, Anita, who had heard the news while working at the aid station and had come running home.

After they had wrapped up Sean's body, she turned to her mother and said, "Mom, I'm going back to the aid station. They need my help."

Carmen sobbed and hugged her. She was proud of her young daughter's fortitude and maturity, and said, "Good, Anita. Go and help the wounded get better."

Chapter 36

It wasn't until that evening that things started to settle down in Sea Breezes. After allowing the families of the dead to grieve, Rich thought it best to pass the word around the community that they would bury their dead at 6 o'clock out in the burial grounds. He knew that after many hours in the afternoon heat of the middle of summer, bodies would become unpleasant to be around. He enlisted two men and a woman who were hanging around the lake area to make the notifications. Among the dead were two adults- one man and one woman- and two children, Sean and the little girl. Four other adults and one child had been wounded. Two of the wounded adults might not make it.

Rich was juggling a lot of balls in the air throughout the day. He drove over to the Carlucci house and asked Fred to organize a grave-digging party. He told him to pick up the dead Zulus' bodies and bury them first. He also told Fred to make sure he and his men searched the bodies for guns and ammo, and anything else useful. He drove over to Donna's house hoping to be able to talk to her about the burial ceremony.

Donna was out in the front yard talking to two of her next-door neighbors, so he stopped and asked her if she would officiate again at the burial ceremony for the residents at six o'clock. She agreed.

Then she asked Rich, "Is there anything else I can help you with between now and then?" Rich's next task was to remove the Zulus' pickup truck that had been shot up near his house, so he said, "As a matter of fact, Donna, you all can give me a hand. Would you help me remove the bodies and the truck from the street near our house?"

They all readily agreed, and jumped in Rich's pickup. He drove back to his house and got a length of rope from his garage, then drove back to the disabled pickup. As he was tying the rope from his rear bumper to the front bumper of the destroyed pickup, the others searched the bodies in the truck's cab and came up with a 5.56 mm rifle and several 30 rd. magazines of ammo. They also got a Taurus 9 mm semi-auto pistol with a couple of magazines from the dead driver. From the two dead Zulu's in the street, they recovered rifle, a pistol, and a shotgun. Donna said to the others, "Hell of a price to pay for getting more guns for us."

They all loaded the bodies into the Zulu's pickup bed, and then Donna steered the vehicle as Rich towed it out the back gate and off to the side near the edge of the tree line. The four hauled the bodies out and dumped them near the back gate where Fred Carlucci's burial team would be sure to see them to pick up and bury.

After he took Donna home, he drove to the aid station to check on Sophia. She was still in surgery so he waited in the house's living room, now used as a waiting room. Twenty minutes later, Dr. Rajan came out of the dining room, saw Rich, and walked over to him.

"Rich, Sophia will be fine. Her Tibia has been nicked, but not broken. I was able to remove the small bone fragments, and sew up the bullet's entry and exit holes. Julia is bandaging her wounds and putting a splint on her leg.

"Barring some serious infection, she should completely recover in six weeks or so, but her leg is going to be too sore to walk on for a few weeks at least.

"She's kind of out of it still, but I'll move her into one of the bedrooms until she recovers. I gave her two hydrocodone tablets so she'll need a couple of hours of rest before she can go home."

"Thanks, Ahmad. I appreciate you working on her. I'll be back in two hours."

"I'll still be here, Rich. I operated earlier on a man and a woman who I'm not sure are going to make it. We triaged the wounded so Sophia's was the last surgery, but I'll be here most of the night. I'll see you in a little bit." Dr. Rajan turned around and headed back into one of the bedrooms to check on his other patients.

Rich had gotten the guard roster from Josh and took it upon himself to start making the necessary changes. He crossed out names, some permanently, and then started filling in other names where he knew the wounded wouldn't be pulling duty for a while, Sophia's name among them. He drove around and made sure the new people were notified in time for the evening shift guard change at 8 p.m. When he was done he drove over to Josh and Carmen's house.

Rich and Josh loaded Sean's body into the back of Josh's pickup, drove out the back gate to the burial ground, and gently laid the body out by an open grave. Josh drove Rich back home, then headed back home himself. They had decided to lower Sean's body into his grave in the presence of all the family together. Twenty minutes later, at 5:45, he went and picked up Josh, Carmen and Anita in his Outback and drove them to the graveyard.

At the ceremony, Donna said a few words of remembrance, but none of the relatives wanted to speak. What could they say? Donna ended the ceremony by leading everyone in reciting the 23rd Psalm. When it was over, the mourners filed back towards the back gate to walk or drive home. Sadly, burials had become all too common.

At 8:20 Rich drove around to each guard position and checked to make sure that they were all manned. They were.

It was dark by the time he got back to the aid station and he carried Sophia into their Outback. Dr. Rajan opened the hatchback door and pulling down a rear seat section so Sophia could lie down flat. They headed home, and Rich carried his wife into the master bedroom and laid her down on their bed.

Sophia was fully awake now, and actually admitted to being hungry, so Rich opened a can of beef and vegetable soup, heated it over the BBQ grill and poured it into two bowls, a little for himself but most of it for Sophia. He brought the bowls into the bedroom and they both ate their supper, Sophia sitting up in the bed, and Rich sitting on a dining room chair next to her. Sophia noticed the difference in the portions but didn't say anything. She knew she needed the nourishment.

After they had finished eating and chatting a bit, Rich went into the kitchen and fed Tasha a piece of beef jerky and added a piece of dried fish. He filled a bucket with water and added a little soap, then washed, rinsed and dried the dishes and put them away. He hugged his dog, let her lick his face again, and then cleaned the blood off of her muzzle. He petted Tasha and said, "Good girl, Tasha. Good girl." Tasha smiled a doggy smile and wagged her tail. She knew she had done good.

Just before bedtime he brought an antibiotic tablet and a hydrocodone capsule Dr. Rajan had given him for Sophia, along with a glass of water. He had to wake her to get her to take the medicine. They talked for a while until Sophia got drowsy again from the medication. Rich helped her lie down flat and rearranged the pillows under her leg to keep it elevated. Sophia fell back asleep almost before he had left the room.

Rich brought in the makeshift chair-toilet and its bucket from the bathroom and set it up beside their bed on Sophia's side, in case she needed to go to the bathroom during the evening. Rich didn't want to risk accidentally hitting her leg during the night so made up a pallet of blankets to sleep on the floor at the foot of the bed so he could hear her, and help her if she needed anything.

At a little after eleven o'clock he lay down on his makeshift bed and fell asleep, exhausted.

Chapter 37

The next morning, Rich helped Sophia with her morning toilet and washing, then he went to the kitchen to make breakfast. They had gotten a box of Cheerios during the last distribution, so it was two cups of dandelion tea and two bowls of Cheerios in water for breakfast. After they had eaten, Rich explained that he had to go to the morning meeting, but first he needed to talk to Donna and go check on the Koenigs to see how they were doing.

He looked at Sophia and said, "Hon, I think we need to go and check out Pelican's Landing to see if the Zulus left anything we could use. I doubt they left much, if anything, but we can't afford not to look."

"Maybe, Rich, but why does it always have to be you and Josh? Why can't someone else lead a scavenging party for a change?"

"Maybe someone could, Sophia, but I'm not about to ask Josh to now. He and I have had the training and experience, and all the things we do now need to be done by whoever is the most capable.

"I don't know anything about gardening, or how to run a trial, and I'm no fisherman, so I don't do any of those things. But I do know how to run combat operations, and I can shoot and observe on roof guard duty, so those are the things I do for the community. The same with Josh. He's also better at the close-in security stuff, so that's what he does."

"Speaking of Josh, Rich, when you go up there, please tell Carmen that if she wants to talk, I'll be glad to listen. You could even drive me up there later on."

"Sophia, you need to stay in bed and rest, and you don't need the risk of falling and injuring your leg. I'll talk to Carmen, but if she wants to talk to you she'll have to come here." Rich took a last sip of his dandelion tea and said, "Listen, I've got to go. Stay in bed and rest, OK?"

Sophia sighed and said, "OK, Rich. I will."

He got her a glass of water and a hydrocodone tablet for her pain, stood there and watched her take it, then left her in bed to rest. He gave her a quick kiss, headed out the front door and walked to Donna's house.

When he got there, Donna was dumping a bucket into her garbage pit. After exchanging greetings, she invited him into the house and they sat down in the living room.

"Rich, I'm sorry to hear about Sophia and especially Sean Koenig. What a terrible thing to happen, and in broad daylight! Is Sophia OK? How are the Koenigs doing?"

"Sophia's in pain, but I think she'll be fine once she heals. I haven't seen the Koenigs since yesterday evening, but I'm heading over there after I talk to you about today's morning meeting."

"OK. What did you have in mind?"

"Well, Donna, I know the community is hurting now, but I think we should go out to Pelican's Landing and see if there's anything there we can scrounge. If we don't get there fast, some of the other scavengers on the island will beat us to it. We both know that there are other small groups out there, since we've been attacked several times by them. I think we need to go out there today. What do you think?"

"I don't know, Rich. Everyone's pretty bummed out about the attack. Here we thought we were almost immune from daylight attacks, but the way it went down, it's obvious that the Zulus did some reconnaissance and planning before they hit us. They knew where the guard posts were, and they knew they needed a large, heavy truck of some kind to clear a path through the blocked entranceway. I'm sure they didn't count on losing as many fighters as they did, not to mention the pickup. They were stupid to try to drive so far into Sea Breezes and that resulted in them staying longer than they probably had planned, and it cost them. I would bet that their leader's plan didn't include sticking around as long as they did. I think they intended to hit us quick and run. It didn't work out that way for them. But it also wasn't very good for us either."

"I know, Donna. Josh and I never figured on a scenario where someone would commandeer a heavy garbage truck to lead an attack against us during daylight hours. Obviously we're going to have to reinforce the entranceway, kind of shutting the barn door after the horses are loose, but it's got to be done."

"I agree, but back to your proposal- I'm not sure the residents are up for another dangerous trip out to an unknown area. What if the Zulus left some people behind in Pelican's Landing?"

"I doubt that, Donna. The bridge observation team said they were loaded up with bags, almost certainly of food and other essentials. That doesn't sound like they were just out for a raid. And I doubt they split their forces up. I suppose it's possible that they had two factions, one that wanted to stay and one that wanted to go, but that's another reason we need to go and check- to see if they're still a threat to the island. If we do see that there are armed guards at the entrance, we won't try to shoot our way in. None of us have the stomach for that."

"Another thing, Rich. If all of the Zulus have left, do you really think they would leave behind anything worthwhile, especially food? I mean, the bridge watchers said they had 25 or 30 people in the convoy and that was after leaving five bodies here."

Rich considered her arguments for a moment, then said, "Yeah, I guess you're right, Donna. Maybe if yesterday's attack hadn't happened we could justify taking the risk. I guess we should put that idea on hold for a while. Thanks for your thoughts on this. You've always had a good perspective on things. Listen, I'm going to go up to the Koenigs' house now. Want to come?"

Not right now, Rich. I've got some cleaning up to do, then I'll head up to the morning meeting. See you there."

"OK, Donna. See you in a bit." Rich left and walked up to the Koenigs' house. It was 8:20 when he got there.

The front door opened, and Josh said, "Come on in, Rich, and sit down. We've got some things to talk about."

"Josh, I'm so sorry about Sean. Are Carmen and Anita doing OK?"

"Anita is, but Carmen's having a rough time of it. Listen, if you're thinking we need to check out Pelican's Landing, that's OK, but I can't go off and leave Carmen now."

"I understand, Josh, but Donna and I talked, and she convinced me that the payoff wouldn't be worth the risk. I guess it's true that they wouldn't have left much of anything of value, and I don't think they split up the gang and left anyone behind. The Werewolves were less than half the size of the Zulus when they pulled out, so they didn't have as many people to feed for as long a time as the Zulus. And that's probably why the Werewolves didn't try too hard to find all the available food in Sunset Beach and take it with them. They had all the food they could carry with them already.

"But that still leaves us with the food problem. People are starting to think that we aren't going to be able to make it. I heard that some people are even weighing the possibility of heading out and trying to drive through Port Monroe and out to the countryside to live, or to find a small town to live in. Actually, I think that's what the Werewolves were planning. They're probably going from small town to small town, raiding and pillaging anything they can find."

"You could be right, Rich. But we're running out of options. All I can see to do is repeat some of the things we've already done. For one, we could go back and try to get a couple of more boats to use for fishing. I'm not sure that'll make a big difference unless we get something big enough to go out a lot farther to find better fishing grounds, and stay out for a couple of days. But, frankly, we're running out of people to do all the things that need to be done.

"By the way, thanks for picking up on getting the guard roster updated and making sure we had roof guards out last night. I wasn't in any shape to worry about those details yesterday.

"If you'll give the roster back to me I'll go over the changes you made last night and try to figure out how we can juggle people for next week. That's about the only thing I'll be doing today, except to be with Carmen."

"I understand, Josh. By the way, Sophia asked me to tell Carmen that if she'd like to just talk to someone to come on down to our house. It might do both of them good."

"Thanks, Rich. Carmen's sleeping now, but when she gets up I'll tell her."

"OK, I'm going to head on over to the meeting. Are you coming?"

"Yes, but I'll be a little late. I want to double check the guard roster for the next couple of days and I probably need to talk to some people and switch around duties. We're due to change over the roof guard duty to the second group at the beginning of next week, and I've got to see whose doing what and if we need to pull anyone off of fishing or gardening."

"Understand. I'll see you over there."

Chapter 38

Rich headed over to the picnic area early to chat with some of the neighbors to get a sense of where their minds were. And it wasn't very positive. What he sensed was resignation and despair. People were hungry, tired and had very little hope that things would get better any time soon. Many were malnourished and others were sick. Some spoke of leaving for the countryside, and others were wondering when and if they would get some help from the government.

At 9, Donna came up to him and said, Rich, I want to start off the meeting today. I need to give them a bit of a pep talk, and I'll also announce that we won't be going out to Pelican's Landing for the foreseeable future, and why. Did you and Josh come up with anything?"

"Well, I'll let Josh talk about it, but he mentioned the idea of going back to Sunset Beach and making an effort to get two of the larger boats started, and use them for overnight and longer distance fishing trips. Hell, it's worth a try. He also needs to make some guard roster adjustments for next week."

"OK. Do you need to say anything?"

"No, I guess it's just you and Josh today. People may want to ask questions and may want to discuss some options they're considering. And maybe someone has an idea we haven't thought of yet. I'll stick around just in case I need to chime in on the feasibility of any suggestions."

"Good. Let's go."

Donna got up on the picnic table they always used and made a very impassioned and uplifting speech about sticking together and doing the best everyone can to help each other. Some of the residents perked up a bit, but it was something they had all heard before. When she told them they wouldn't be going out to Pelican's Landing, there was a mixture of relief over not taking on another dangerous outing, and disappointment that there would be no prospect for another scavenging opportunity to get more food.

Josh got up next and started off with getting some of the more mechanically-minded guys to go back to Sunset Beach and try to get a couple of big boats started, in order to increase the fishing opportunities. That got quite a bit of support. Then Josh went into trying to get the guard rosters juggled and filled out with names and assignments. That brought out some negative reactions from disappointed people.

One woman, the mother of the little girl and boy that were shot yesterday said angrily, "The fuckin' guards didn't help us out yesterday. Why waste our time?" A few others murmured agreement.

Rich knew the woman's name was Edna something, but he couldn't remember her last name. He looked over at Josh, who was turning red with anger and decided he'd better say something quickly to turn the temperature down.

He looked at the angry woman and said, "Edna, I'm very sorry for your loss. I hope your son is doing OK, and from what I heard at the aid station, he'll fully recover. But actually, the roof guards did do a lot for us yesterday. They provided early warning that gave us time to get our weapons, and all of them, except for Louise Goldman, who got hit at the beginning of the raid at the entrance, were able to fire back at the attackers. Had they not opened fire the raiders would have killed more people. Sean Koenig paid for that with his life. If you want to be angry with someone, blame me. I never thought to plan for someone using a heavy vehicle to break through our barricade."

Several people nodded their heads, and Edna was somewhat mollified. But she turned around and stalked off anyway.

Rich couldn't blame her. These were shitty circumstances, and she had just lost one child and another had been wounded.

Another man asked a question and he asked it calmly, trying to bring some peace to the meeting. "Rich, Donna, we're thinking of trying to get a small group together and head out to the countryside. We figure we might be able to find a small town, or at least a safer place in the woods to try to live off the land if we have to. Maybe in the woods we can find some domesticated animals on the loose or some wild game to eat."

Donna decided to take that one. "I know several of you have been considering doing that, but just think about it for a minute. You'd have to run the gauntlet of getting through Port Monroe, and that includes evading the gangs, and maybe even the Army, who won't have any idea who you are. What if one or more of those groups has the roads blocked?

And even if you do make it through the city, how will you decide which way to go? You don't know anything about the status of the small towns around us. For all you know, you might find yourself in a town where the Werewolves or the Zulus have set up. Do you think you'll be able to negotiate your way past them or any other hostile elements? Do you think the people in any surviving small towns are going to receive you with open arms when they probably don't have enough to eat either?

"No one can stop your or anyone else from leaving, but you'd better think long and hard about the dangers before you do." That quieted everyone down, so Donna continued. "Look, here in Sea Breezes we have the fishermen, the gardeners, and the aid station. We may not have perfect security here, but it certainly has been good enough to protect most of us. You all know that if it hadn't been for the roof guards and the QRF teams we all would have been killed a long time ago. Personally I'm not going to be leaving Sea Breezes on a wild goose chase out to find some country nirvana that doesn't exist."

That pretty much ended the discussion so Josh stood up and started talking about the guard roster and who was going to volunteer to go to Sunset Beach and try to get a couple of larger cruisers. When Josh finished, the meeting broke up and everyone went back to their usual routines.

Chapter 39

Rich walked with Donna on the way back to their houses. "Donna, you did some good with your speech. I think it helped lift their spirits a bit. God knows we all need that. I especially liked the dose of reality you gave to the folks who're thinking about striking out for the countryside." He looked at her with a smile on his face and said, "Hell, you even convinced me to stick around."

Donna grinned back at him and said, "Thanks, Rich. I'm glad that Josh is busy working on finding people to get the security rosters up to date. It's something to do that'll take his mind off the loss of his son. How's Carmen doing, by the way?"

"I don't know, Donna. I didn't see her this morning. Josh said she was sleeping, and I hope she was. He also said she wasn't coping too well and told me that if we planned to go out to Pelican's Landing, he wouldn't be going. He's feeling it too, and he obviously isn't going to be taking any more unnecessary risks that might leave Carmen mourning her husband as well as her child.

"And believe me, I understand. Sophia's only wounded and I had misgivings about leaving her. I'm just trying to figure out if there is anything else we could do to survive. One crazy idea I had was to take a boat and cross over into north Port Monroe and try to make our way through town over to the airport and contact the military. The problem with that is that we might not make it through whoever controls that part of the city, and even if we get there, the Army might just turn us around. You know they've got the hands full trying to figure out what they need to do at the port and the oil refinery, not to mention figuring out how to establish some sort of military and civilian security and control over the city. I really doubt that they're in the rescue business yet."

"Yeah, that does sound kind of crazy. But you know, if something doesn't happen soon, it might be worth a try as a last ditch effort, if we really get desperate."

"The thing is, Donna, I'm not so sure we aren't that desperate now. The only other thing, aside from trying to expand our fishing, is to go out to that group of houses where Leroy used to live and see if we can find anything. We never did make it back there."

"Not today or even tomorrow, Rich. People need some down time. Josh is going to try to get a team together to go and get us another couple of large motor boats. Let's see how that goes before we start reaching for more risky measures. The last thing we need right now is to lose some more neighbors."

"Yeah, Donna, you're right. I'd better go check on Sophia, then swing by the aid station and see how the wounded are doing."

"OK, Rich. Give Sophia my best. Take care."

Donna watched him for a few seconds as he walked back down the street and sighed, shaking her head at herself.

Chapter 40

August was coming to an end with no other major events or problems occurring. Jacob Hanson, "Captain" Martin Goldman, and Fred Carlucci took a truck with two armed guards and went back to Sunset Beach. They had decided to spend the night in the marina if they couldn't get any boats started the first day, and that's what they ended up doing. They kept one man on guard at the front gate at all times, and during the night they rotated the duty every four hours.

They spent most of the first day looking for keys on the boats, and even checked some of the condo apartments looking in obvious key-keeping places, such as in small drawers or on key hooks behind doors. That was the easiest solution so they tried that first. After looking all morning, they gave up and started to work on hot-wiring a boat or two.

No one had had any experience hot wiring vehicles, much less cabin cruisers, and all those adventure and cop movies that made hot wiring look easy were obviously B.S., at least in modern vehicles and boats. Using trial and error, they burned up a couple of batteries and the electrical circuit on one cruiser. But they learned from their mistakes and finally got one large cruiser to start. That was great, but they hadn't thought to check the gas tank first and only after it fired up did they see from the fuel gauge that the boat had almost no fuel in it- and it turned out to be a diesel engine.

So they scrounged up an empty 5-gallon gas can and went around to the other boats looking for one that ran on diesel. They found one and were able to siphon about eight gallons out of it. They added that to the tank and hoped it would be enough to get them back to the Sea Breezes "marina" where the other boats were anchored.

Jacob, especially, did not want to give up with just one boat, and argued for sticking around a third day to keep working on finding keys or hot wiring another boat. They compromised and spent the second morning and early afternoon trying, but all they accomplished was burning out another boat's electrical circuit, so they gave up. Jacob and Fred piloted the boat they had been able to start, out and around the north edge of the island, and over to the northeast side where the other Sea Breezes boats were. The problem was that they hadn't thought to find a dinghy and take it with them to get to shore with. They were too excited about getting the boat back to Sea Breezes and getting home. Of course, the dinghy they did have was already on the shore, so the two ended up swimming from the boat to the where the dinghy was, laughing at their own oversight.

The three other men and woman drove the truck back, reported in to Josh, and told him what they had accomplished. Now all they had to do was to go out the next day to one of the filling stations and tap a storage tank with diesel fuel so they could fill up the boat's fuel tank. They had several smaller gas containers and they designated one more to use only for diesel.

They discovered that there was only one large pickup in the community that ran on diesel, so they filled that one to the brim and used it as a source to siphon fuel into the two five gallon cans.

They spent most of the next day shuttling cans of diesel from the truck parked on the edge of Phase II, back and forth through the woods, to the dinghy, and then out to the boat. The cans were heavy, and Martin had thought to use a wheelbarrow to carry two fuel cans per trip. It took them the rest of the day, but the next morning they had the big diesel boat topped off, as well as both of the gasoline boats.

After getting the second cruiser they had two large boats that together could go far out into the gulf, and one small motorboat for closer-in fishing. They didn't bother using the rowboat and canoes anymore- that had always been a time-consuming and low yield venture anyway.

After the first day of getting used to operating the two big cruisers together, and coordinating which areas to go to each morning and how long the boats would stay out, they had been able to almost double the amount of fish brought in, and that was a great help to the community.

But everyone was really getting tired of eating only fish and a few vegetables from the garden. Their bodies craved carbohydrates, and there just weren't many carbohydrates to eat, except for the little they found in the fruit and vegetables they ate infrequently in small proportions. People with diets that were used to a lot of pasta, cookies, and bread products were having a hard time adjusting.

At least there had been no other incidents in the last couple of weeks. But, Rich and Josh were planning another scavenging trip out to Leroy's old neighborhood.

Chapter 41

The next morning, Greg and Rebecca Gibson were out on bridge observation duty and at 10:45 Rebecca noticed movement on the bridge. She elbowed her husband, who had nodded off, and said, "Hey, Greg! Wake up! We got company."

Greg's eyes shot open and he grabbed for his rifle. "What? Where?"

"Out there on the hump of the bridge. Looks like a small truck or something. Wait. Now I see two of them."

Greg picked up the binoculars and said, "Those aren't just trucks, those are Humvees! The Army must be checking out the island."

"What should we do, Greg?"

"Josh told us that if the Army ever came out we needed to show ourselves and tell them what's going on. So, I'm going to leave my rifle here and go out and stand in the road and wave my arms. You call Josh and let him know."

"OK, hand me your walkie-talkie." He did and she called, "Josh this is Rebecca at the bridge, Post #6, come in." She repeated the call twice before she got a response.

"This is Josh, what's up, Rebecca?"

"We just spotted a couple of Humvees heading our way. Greg went out and is standing in the middle of the road slowly waving his arms. I don't know whether or not the Humvees have seen him yet. OK, wait, maybe they have. They've slowed down and it looks like some kind of machinegun on top of the lead vehicle is now pointing at him. Holy shit!"

"Rebecca, go on out there with him- no weapons, and no sudden movements. I'll get Rich and we'll be right there."

"OK, Josh, I'm going. Hurry." She left her rifle and took her pistol out of her belt, grabbed the walkie-talkie, and walked out and stood by her husband. She had a dark thought. "What if some gang had captured the two Army vehicles? Well, I guess we'll know in a minute"

Chapter 42

"Hey, Ell Tee, looks like a couple of people standing in the road on the other side of the bridge. What do you want me to do?"

"Slow down, Thompson. Zeke, get your gun sights on those two. Don't fire unless you're fired upon."

"WILCO, Ell Tee."

Lieutenant (LT) Debbie Johansen was a First Lieutenant in the 82nd Airborne Division. She was in the lead vehicle with her driver, Corporal Lou Thompson. Sergeant Elmo Zachariah, "Zack," was her gunner. In the back seat was Corporal Delgado, additional security, armed with an M-4 rifle. In the vehicle behind her was Staff Sergeant Raul Martinez in charge of his crew in the second Humvee, call sign Two Bravo.

"Two Bravo, this is Two Alfa, do you see what I'm seeing?"

"Affirmative, Alpha. Take it easy. I can't pull around you because it looks like we're coming to that part of the bridge that is one way due to the damaged lane, so be careful."

"WILCO, Bravo, stay alert."

Lieutenant Johansen clicked on her internal microphone and said, "Thompson, approach slowly. Stop about 50 meters away from the man and woman and keep your engine running."

"WILCO, Ell Tee."

As the vehicles slowed down, Rebecca looked over at Greg and said out of the corner of her mouth, "I wish they'd point that machinegun somewhere else. It scares the shit out of me."

"No, it's OK, Rebecca. They're just being careful. Don't move, and don't say anything. I'll try to talk to them when they get closer."

Lieutenant Johansen turned around and said, "Delgado, come with me and keep your rifle at the ready, but don't point it at them. I don't want to scare them or provoke a shooting incident."

"Yes, Ma'am."

Lieutenant Johansen and Corporal Delgado approached the man and woman. When they got within hearing distance, Lieutenant Johansen said, "Identify yourselves."

Greg responded, "I'm Greg Gibson and this is my wife, Rebecca. We're from the Sea Breezes development here on Phelps Island, and we've been on lookout here on the bridge."

Lieutenant Johansen turned to Corporal Delgado beside her and said, "Search them."

It was obvious the two soldiers had done this drill before. He handed his rifle to the Lieutenant and told the Gibsons to get down on the ground face down and spread their arms out. He did a thorough search and then had them roll over and he repeated the process, while Lieutenant Johansen drew her pistol and aimed it at the pair. He looked up at the Lieutenant and said, "They're clean, ma'am."

She looked at the Gibsons and said, "OK, you can stand up and relax now. And you can put your arms down. Sorry about that, but we've learned to trust no one out here. Are you the guys that laid that big HELP sign out in the dirt of that open field?"

Greg smiled, and said, "Yes, that's us. Man, ... er, I mean, ma'am, are we ever glad to see you. We have a couple of our leaders coming out to talk with you, so if you see a vehicle approaching, they're with us, and they're not hostile."

"Thanks for telling me, Mr. Gibson, because I see someone coming now. I hope it's one of yours." She turned half way around and yelled, "SGT Zachariah, hold your fire. I think that's a friendly approaching, but stay alert." She saw him nod and heard, "Yes, ma'am."

She turned back to the Gibsons and asked, "About how many of you are there in Sea Breezes?"

"Actually, we know exactly, and so does everyone else, because we distribute all food and supplies that we get per person. We have 197 men women and children. So far we've lost 53 of the original residents since before the Collapse. Some of those never came home from work in Port Monroe after that first day, and the rest were either away from home, killed in firefights or died of sickness. We've had a couple of suicides also."

Lieutenant Johansen was amazed. They hadn't run into anyone in Port Monroe except gang members since they arrived, much less an organized community that was still surviving. She looked up and saw two men getting out of a pickup and walk towards her. She was glad to see both approach unarmed and with their hands up, but she looked at them and said, "Both of you, please stop where you are and identify yourselves."

Rich complied. He squinted his eyes and saw the First Lieutenant insignia sewed on her uniform and said, "Lieutenant, I'm Rich Cantrell, Lieutenant Colonel, U.S. Army, retired. This is Gunnery Sergeant Josh Koenig, U.S. Marines, retired. Can you tell us who you are?"

Lieutenant Johansen ignored the question and said, "Do either of you have any I.D. on you?"

Rich replied, "Yes, Lieutenant, I have my military ID in my billfold. I'll take it out slowly and bring it to you. He did so, and Lieutenant Johansen cautiously took it from him. Rich stepped back a few paces as she examined his ID. She didn't salute as she handed it back, but she did switch to calling him, "sir."

"Sir, I'm First Lieutenant Debbie Johansen, assistant S-2 of the 1st Bn., 509th Airborne. That's assistant intelligence officer.

Rich smiled and said, "Thanks Lieutenant. I believe I still remember what S-2 stand for."

Lieutenant Johansen actually blushed a little, but she smiled and said, "Well, yes sir, of course. We were brought back from Europe and attached to the 82nd. They sent us straight to Ft. Benning instead of Ft. Bragg and re-equipped us there. Our Charlie Company was flown in to Port Monroe to secure the airport, and the rest of the battalion arrived later.

"I've been sent out to the island to do a quick recon of the area. We were all puzzled by who had set out the HELP sign, and whether it was a trap or not. So, how have you guys survived when everyone else didn't?"

Rich answered her with a quick summary of the sequence of events they had endured since the Collapse, from getting the community organized, to the various attacks against them, including by both the Zulus and the Werewolves, and about what they had done to try to survive- the scavenging trips, the fishing, the garden, and so forth. Rich noted that as soon as he began the story, Lieutenant Johansen had taken out a notebook and a pocket recorder to capture what he said.

Rich finished with, "I want to make a few things very clear, Lieutenant. We have taken no hostile action against anyone who didn't attack us first. We never took anything from anyone who was alive, and we've rescued several people we've found and brought them into our community."

When he had finished, the Lieutenant said, "That's a remarkable story, sir. Do you believe that there are any gang members left on the island?"

"We're not sure, Lieutenant, but it's not likely. We almost wiped out the Werewolves, and I'm pretty sure all of the Zulus are gone now, although as I mentioned, we haven't been out to Pelican's Landing to verify that because of the high risk/reward probability. There's a small possibility that the Zulus left a few people behind, but I don't think so.

"We do know that there are several small, armed groups roaming around the island, most of whom probably were decent enough citizens until they were driven by desperation to killing and looting. But I see no threats to your unit from Phelps Island. Everyone left here is just concentrating on staying alive, and we're all afraid to go into the city for fear of the gangs."

"Thank you Colonel. That's what I was sent out to determine, and it's good to know. We've been struggling a bit with the armed gangs in Port Monroe, especially the damn MS-13."

"So, Lieutenant, what's going on, security wise, for you guys? I assume your unit is here primarily to analyze the status of the port, airport and refinery, and that you have encountered some obstacles."

"That's correct, sir. The MS-13 gang had pretty much taken over the city, and they are the most ruthless savages I've ever seen. They've absorbed a few men and women from other gangs who were willing to join them and killed the rest, usually by chopping off limbs and heads. We think the Zulus have joined up with them, or at least know some of them did anyway. We've had several run-ins with MS-13 since we've been here. They tried to probe our advanced party and they took some heavy casualties for their efforts. They've also ambushed some of our convoys when they drove out to recon the refinery. But they paid a pretty good price by trying to come up against machineguns, automatic M-4 rifles, and our new shoulder-fired MAAWS rocket launchers. But they're still around, and still a threat, especially from sniper fire."

"Well, Lieutenant, obviously the big question we have is, can you help us? Since your Charlie Company first landed we've been hoping for some help from your unit. We're all malnourished, to the point that some have lost their minds, given up, and committed suicide. We heard on the HAM radio broadcast from the president that some areas would begin getting some government relief soon."

"I'm sorry, sir, but that's not part of our mission, at least not yet. We still need to establish control of Port Monroe, and until we do, providing relief and rescue to civilians is not something we're equipped for, or supplied to do. But, I'll take your information back to my boss and the battalion commander, and let him know what's going on out here."

"Thank you, Lieutenant. Any help at all we can get in the way of food will save some lives. By the way, is there any chance you could loan us a radio so we can keep in touch with your unit?"

Lieutenant Johansen paused, and said, "Sir I don't have any spare radios with me, and I don't have authorization to leave you one anyway. I'll go back and lay all of this out for my boss and he can talk to the battalion commander. I'll see what we can do, sir, but it will be up to the C.O."

Rich, sighed and said, "Thanks, Lieutenant. That's all I can ask. Just tell them that there are some good Americans starving out here, and we could use some help." Rich almost blushed from laying the patriotism on so thick but, by God, it was true.

"Yes sir. I understand. All I can say is that I'll present your case to my boss and give him my recommendations."

"Good enough, Lieutenant. You said your name was Debbie Johansen?"

"Yes sir."

"OK, thank you for coming out here and listening to our situation, Lieutenant. By the way, you said you were from the 1st Bn., 509th. Is your unit at full strength?

She hesitated at the question and then decided that he was a safe enough person to give out a few details to. He certainly wasn't part of any hostile force. "No sir, but we have some Florida National Guard personnel and equipment to help flesh us out. In all we have around 600 soldiers in the battalion, plus they sent along some engineers and other specialists to look at the port and the refinery. We're good enough though, sir.

Rich smiled and said, Yes, Lieutenant, I'm sure you are."

"Anyway, thank you, sir, for all the info about the situation here on the island. And good luck to you all." She snapped off an unexpected salute to Rich, and in a pure muscle memory reaction, he returned it smartly. She walked back to her Humvee, got in and had her vehicles turn a circle around them, then headed back over the bridge.

Rebecca looked at Rich and said, "Well, Rich, what do you think?"

All eyes were on him and he said, "I don't really know, guys. She's sympathetic, but I understand that her battalion is not in the business of providing relief to civilians. We'll still probably have to wait a long while yet."

Rich said to both of the Gibson's, "Good observation and reaction guys. You did everything right by being alert and stopping the Humvees. I think it's safe for you to come on back with us. I don't expect any more coming and going across the bridge today. You might as well have a little down time."

Greg smiled and said, "OK, Rich. We'll see you back at the ranch."

Chapter 43

Word of the encounter at the bridge had gotten around the community and at the next morning meeting everyone was abuzz. Rumors were flying around like bees, most of them based on hope and conjecture, but nevertheless it was certainly a more positive crowd at the picnic area than anyone had seen since after the return from Sunset Beach.

Rich hated to throw any cold water on their optimism, but he had to make sure they were realistic as well as hopeful. He began the meeting by relating a summary of what had gone on the day before at the bridge. He didn't sugar coat anything nor did he dash all hope. But, he was honest in saying that no promises had been made, and that the Lieutenant had made it clear that civilian rescue was not part of the battalion's mission.

Kathryn Brown was there with her son, Malcolm and asked the big question outright. "Rich, what do you think they'll do for us, if anything?"

"Kathryn, I really don't know. The good thing is that there is now a record and a report about us heading up the chain of command, but as it proceeds higher, details of our little situation will eventually be cut out by summaries of bigger problems.

"But at least the battalion commander will be made aware of our dire situation, and we can only hope he does something that will help us. Lieutenant Johansen probably got her boss, the S-2 intelligence officer, to listen to the recording of my description of what we had been through, and he or she'll probably summarize it for the battalion commander. It all depends on whether the battalion staff and the battalion commander decide if they can do anything about our situation, and I don't have a crystal ball on that."

That honest conclusion let the air out of the bubble a bit, but at least everyone had a little hope now. Rich continued, "Remember that at 10 we're going out on a scavenging trip back to the area where Leroy used to live. There will only be three pickups going this time, so those of you who have volunteered, start lining up at Josh's house at 9:50. I don't expect us to be gone long."

There wasn't much of anything else going on that day other than the scavenging trip, so the meeting broke up and everyone went back to work. Rich went from the meeting to the aid station as he hadn't gotten an update on the sick and wounded in several days. Dr. Rajan had mostly good news.

"As you know Rich, we lost one of the seriously wounded, but the other is hanging on and it looks like she might survive. I just can't say for sure right now. All of the other wounded are home and recovering. We haven't had any more cases of Cholera, and just the usual amount of diarrhea and minor illnesses. One thing I am grateful for is that we haven't had a flu epidemic. In everyone's weakened condition, it would have hit the community very hard. Knock on wood."

"All of that's good to hear, Ahmad. How's your family doing?"

"They are well, Rich. Aisha is working in the garden and the boys are helping her. My oldest wants to be a roof guard, but I told him the minimum age was 16. He is two years away, so hopefully he will never have to serve." Ahmad smiled when he had finished and Rich said, "God help us if he does, Ahmad."

Chapter 44

They pulled out of Sea Breezes right on time and in less than 10 minutes they were back at Leroy's house. They set up their defenses around the truck with the drivers, and the rest of the party went house to house, first putting a guard out one house down from where they were searching, as well as front and back as security behind each house before they knocked on the door. No one ever answered.

They got down to where they had rescued Charlotte, and found nothing but a few cans of food. Rich wondered if they would find much of anything else of use today. In the next to the last house on the street, they found a stash of four cases of microwavable meals, consisting of various entrees such as spaghetti and meatballs, chili con carne, and beef or chicken with something, hidden under the bed in the master bedroom. There were two bodies lying in the bed, and it was obvious they had been victims of an attack, not a suicide. There were no weapons near them and, they had been shot several times in the torso. But whoever had broken into the house and killed its occupants had neglected to look under the bed of the dead couple, probably wanting to avoid the gore.

Aside from some newspapers, batteries and a few other items from that house and some of the other ones, the four cases of microwavables and the few cans of food were all they got- 96 entrees and 4 cans of food- about one for every two people. Rich wondered how in the hell they would distribute that little windfall.

By the next morning meeting, Josh had come up with the solution. He announced that lunch that day would be at the picnic area. So, in two shifts, the first starting at noon and the second at 12:30, people came to the picnic area, sat on the tables and grass with a plate and spoon, and Donna, Carmen, and Kathryn Brown went around with a meal or can of food in each hand. Each family or individual could select a preference for which meal of the two they got for their 1/2 portion, and that would be that. No arguing, no whining, no asking for different selections. If they wanted to swap their chicken and potatoes with someone for their spaghetti and meatballs, then that was up to them. Several people actually did that, to mutual satisfaction. All things considered, it was a fair way to divide up the food, and everyone got a few bites of something different to eat that week, not to mention some of the carbohydrates they all craved.

Sophia was hobbling around with the use of a crutch and sat down at one of the picnic tables. Carmen got her own half portion, walked over, and sat down next to her. She looked down at her meager portion of chili con carne and said, "Well, I guess we should be thankful for small blessings." Sophia smiled and took a bite of her beef stroganoff, savoring every morsel.

Chapter 45

Two days later, around 8 a.m., a helicopter flew over Sea Breezes and flew a couple of laps in a circle around the community. Rich ran outside and quickly saw what was happening. Even if he hadn't, he heard his walkie-talkie squawk and heard the roof guard on the northeast corner, Post #4, calling Josh to tell him that it looked like a helicopter was landing. Josh had answered and Rich knew he was on his way to the helicopter pad.

Rich ran out the back entrance gate towards the helicopter pad and stood there in plain view waving his arms to let the pilot know there was someone on site, waiting, and that it was safe to land. He turned his back, covered his ears, and closed his eyes from the fierce downdraft as the big chopper sat down on the pad. By the time the Blackhawk helicopter had set down, about a dozen people had arrived.

Once on the ground, Rich ducked his head and approached the pilot. The pilot handed him an envelope addressed to "LTC Cantrell", and he heard the pilot tell his crew chief on the headset mike, "OK, Sergeant, unload the MRE's down to these people."

Rich motioned for others to come towards the chopper and they began shuttling cases of MRE's off the helicopter. The blades kept turning so it was obvious the Blackhawk had no intention of shutting down. There were 50 cases offloaded in just a few minutes to the smiling and laughing men and women who were each grabbing a case and stacking them on a nearby concrete foundation. The crew chief took off his helmet and motioned Rich over. Rich noticed he was a Staff Sergeant.

"Are you Lieutenant Colonel Cantrell?"

"Yes, Sergeant, I am."

"Well, I'm Staff Sergeant Sinkovich, sir and this is from the 1st Bn., 509th Airborne. The battalion commander sends his greetings and congratulations on toughing things out, and he asks you to keep this radio that's on the battalion logistical net in case you really need to contact us. Please stay off the net unless you have a true emergency."

Rich grabbed the small tactical radio and said, "Roger, Sergeant Sinkovich. And thank you. You don't know how much this means to us."

Sergeant Sinkovich smiled, saluted and said, "All the way, sir!"

Rich's eyes got teary as he snapped off a return salute and answered with the traditional response, "Airborne!"

Rich backed away, the crew chief gave the pilot a thumb's up, and the chopper pilot lifted off, nosed over into the wind, and climbed away, heading back to the airport.

Rich looked at the note. It was from the battalion commander, Lieutenant Colonel Robert Marchione. It said,

"LTC Cantrell, I served with you a long time ago in the 82nd when I was a young Lieutenant. I remember you well, and I'm glad to be able to help out a fellow Ranger. All of my soldiers are on restricted rations of one or two MRE's, alternating every other day, per soldier. Today was a two-meal day, and every man and woman in the battalion gave up one of their meals today to send them out to you and your people. We've reported your story to brigade headquarters back in Ft. Benning, and asked for additional rations for you. Even if it's approved, it may take awhile, but hang in there. I'm glad to still see that "Rangers Lead The Way!"

Respectfully,

LTC Robert E. Marchione"

Rich sat down on the edge of the concrete foundation that he and a few others had painted with the big white H with a white circle around it. His emotions were running high with old memories and gratitude. He put his hands to his face, and cried tears of relief.

Chapter 46

It was almost pandemonium at the nine o'clock meeting. Rich had gotten several neighbors to load the MRE's in their cars and pickups to take them directly to the picnic area. Everyone had seen or heard the helicopter land, and except for the roof guards, most of them came to the meeting to hear what news it brought.

Rich got everyone quieted down and gave them the details of what had happened. He read them the letter from the battalion commander and some of the men and women got tears in their eyes also.

Rich also told them about the radio, but he cautioned everyone, "They gave us this radio for emergencies only, but they made it clear that this isn't to be used every time we need something. So please understand- we haven't been 'rescued' yet. We just have a 911 number to call now and it will be used only for extreme emergencies.

"That said, we have 600 complete MRE meals, and we're going to hand out one per person after this meeting."

He added before anyone could complain, "I talked to Dr. Rajan on the way up here, and he strongly recommended we use these meals as a supplement to our diet, and not eat them by themselves, or all at once.

"He doesn't want us to upset our digestive systems with a lot of high calorie and spicy food that our stomachs aren't used to.

"That makes sense from a practical perspective also, because we literally still don't know where our next meals are coming from, nor do we know if or when we'll get any more MRE's. We'll have about 400 meals left after today's distribution. We'll store the rest in Donna's house and distribute them, one for each person once a week, for the next two weeks. That's the best way to integrate the MRE's into our diet to keep us going a while.

"Folks, remember, everything else stays the same for us. I wish we felt comfortable enough to lift the roof guard duty during daylight hours, as we had planned to do some day, but after the Zulu attack in broad daylight, I think it would be irresponsible to do that, at least for now."

He paused a minute and asked, "Donna, Josh, anything to add?' They both shook their heads no, so the meeting was adjourned. Everyone made two lines and Carmen and Sophia handed out the meals, checking off their names from the well-worn roster of residents. Donna said she'd take the remaining cases and store them in her spare bedroom. They counted the MRE meals left, and let everyone know the number so they would feel comfortable that no one was skimming.

Chapter 47

The next few weeks went pretty well for Sea Breezes, with no major problems springing up. After a lot of discussion, they finally decided to send three trucks out to Pelican's Landing, primarily to see if there were any Zulus remaining there. Pelican's Landing was on the southeast corner of the island and several homes had been burned or damaged when the oil tanker in the bay off the coast of the refinery had exploded.

Rich led the recon party, and Donna came along also as his #2. She was a good replacement for Josh, who elected to stay behind. Rich wasn't going to take any chances though. If they found guards posted, or if they were fired at, they would carefully and quickly retreat. No one wanted to get into another shootout. Rich dismounted everyone long before they got to the main gate and they approached slowly and cautiously. They saw that the gate was open, but they weren't going to assume anything. Rich hailed anyone who was inside and told them they didn't come looking for trouble. There was no answer from the entrance area, so they entered the gates into the community, and repeated hailing at the houses near the entrance. There was no answer at any of the homes they hailed.

They approached each home, damaged or not, the same way they did when they had checked out other communities- two security guards, front and back, a knock on the door and a shout out, then enter, secure, and scrounge.

Donna's conclusion that the mission had a low reward potential had been accurate and he made it a point to tell her so. "Donna, you were right when you said the Zulus probably used up or carried away all of the food. The dwindling food supply here was probably one of the reasons they left the island when they did. And we haven't found much of anything of use here."

"Thanks, Rich. I wish I had been wrong, but at least we know that all of the Zulus are gone, and that our threat situation is considerably lower now. About the only thing we have to worry about are the small bands of looters roaming around. I have no idea how many of them there are, but I bet they won't be bothering us. I'm sure the word has gotten around these last few months that Sea Breezes had best be left alone. Every group that's tried, large or small, took a real beating."

"I think you're right about that too, Donna. Josh and I have been talking about a plan to cut down on the security demands we've placed on everyone. We'll be smart about it, but I think it can be done.

"Good, Rich. But I wonder what happened to the people who used to live here?"

"I saw that one of the burned-out homes was set deliberately. The walls were made of stone so you could tell the house wasn't damaged by the tanker that was blown up back in February, and it wasn't close to the water anyway. I went down to check it out with a couple of members of my team and it was a pretty gruesome sight. We saw a lot of charred remains of bodies inside, I would guess 40 or more, stacked up on the ground floor. They probably doused them and everything in the home with gasoline and lit it on fire.

I wouldn't recommend anyone else going down there- it's not a pleasant sight, or smell. As for the rest, I imagine the Zulus either let them leave their homes, like the Werewolves did, or maybe they were able to escape. Who knows?"

"Well, I guess there's nothing more we can do here, Rich. Why don't we head on home?"

"Good idea." Rich turned around and yelled for everyone to mount up.

Chapter 48

After Rich and Donna brought back the news that all of the Zulus were gone, Josh came up with a new security plan that would be less manpower intensive than the current one. Josh explained the plan the next evening to Donna and Rich, at a meeting at Donna's house. He had a hand drawn map of the island with main roads indicated. "OK, we're here at the top of this pear-shaped island, and there are no houses to our north and none to our west and east. There were going to be some eventually, I'm sure, like Phase II had been planned, but right now, every home or building is to our south. If we were to clear away the sparse woods to our immediate east and west for about 50 yards, we could open up lines of sight for the roof guards on the southern corners, almost down to the island's east and west shores.

"We could remove the two guard posts at the northern corners and make just one in the center to guard against an attack through Phase II, since any attackers would have to get by the southern guards first. Clear out a few more trees near the entranceway and they could also see anyone approaching from the main entrance road to the south, and we could eliminate the entrance guard too. We've already doubled the cars blocking the entranceway, so no vehicle can get in, not even a garbage truck. Removing two guard posts would reduce our guard commitment by six shifts every day.

"That would also accomplish another critical need- getting everyone's wood supplies stocked up for the winter. Last winter, just from February on, residents cut down most of the trees here in the community, and we're all going to need a lot more wood this winter since we've had cold weather here as early as October before. And that's only a few weeks away."

Rich nodded his head and said, "Josh, a month ago I would have thought you were losing your marbles, but it sounds like a workable plan to me. The only threat we have is the occasional small group, or if gang members were to attack us from across the bridge. But with our bridge watchers, we'd be alerted in time if that happened. The only thing I would change is to make the bridge guys 24/7, and change the shifts a dawn and at dusk."

Donna said, "I agree with that. I say let's make those changes. Our neighbors need a break from the stress, and with all of the MRE's gone we could certainly use a reduction in our workload.

Josh added, "There's one other thing we could do, but I'm not sure we should do it. I heard about this from Leroy, who told me the Viet Cong used them in Vietnam. We could put out some "foot poppers" along the approaches to Sea Breezes on our east and west sides to prevent anyone from crossing northward in areas the southern roof guards can't see."

Donna got a quizzical look on her face and asked, "Josh, what on earth are these "foot popper" things?"

"Well, they're a kind of home-made land mine, and are very simple to make. You take a small piece of wood and drive a nail or screw into it so the tip sticks out about an eighth of an inch. Then you glue a PVC pipe, or some other kind of pipe or small cylinder, onto the base with the nail sticking up in the center.

"The pipe should be just a quarter inch shorter than a shotgun shell around the point of the nail. You dig a small hole and put the piece of wood with the PVC pipe into the hole with the point of the nail facing up inside the PVC pipe. Then you place a shotgun shell with the primer cap resting on the point of the nail, and fill the hole up with dirt, so the top of the shell is just barely above ground level. To make it completely weatherproof you can put a zip lock baggie over the whole contraption and disguise it with loose dirt or leaves sprinkled on top.

"If someone steps on it, theoretically, the impact of a footstep forces the shotgun shell down quickly onto the point of the nail, and that ignites the primer cap so the shell fires upwards, usually taking a foot off, or doing more damage to the body above it. I've never actually seen one of these used myself, but they should work most of the time."

Donna looked over at Rich shaking her head. Rich said, "Yeah I've heard about those types of improvised land mines. Supposedly the Viet Cong used them and several other versions in the Vietnam War. That was before my time so I can't vouch for the reliability of foot poppers, but as Josh said, they should work at least sometimes if they're stepped on. I just don't think we ought to be setting up land mines in an area where someone not intending to do us any physical harm may accidentally cross."

Josh said, "Yeah, I tend to agree, but it was just something I thought I'd mention."

Donna said, "OK, then let's forget about foot poppers and just do the roof guard changes."

At the next morning meeting, Josh announced the new roof guards plan to murmurs of approval. He tacked up the new guard roster for everyone to check.

They decided to leave all of the sandbags up on the roofs of the three prior guard posts-if there were another attack of some sort, people could scramble up the same ladders and have some cover to shoot down on any attackers.

Rich had turned on the radio the battalion had given him from time to time, but most of the chatter on the logistic net had to do with getting reports from the refinery and the port, and boring requests for different types of supplies or ammunition from the line companies. But something else had caught his attention. There seemed to be a buildup of ammunition being sent out to the line companies, and one of the companies had apparently requested some attack helicopter support. He never caught any dates being discussed, but something was up. Just what that was, Rich could only guess.

Chapter 49

Rich didn't have to wait long to find out. At first light the next morning he heard automatic weapons fire coming from downtown Port Monroe, followed by more explosions. It was obvious that the battalion was attacking the city gangs in their hideouts. When strongholds were found, Apache gunships lifted off from the airport and strafed them with their 30 mm automatic cannon. They didn't use their more powerful rockets or missiles because they didn't want to turn parts of the city into rubble.

As soon as Rich had figured out what must be happening, he radioed Josh on his walkie-talkie and said, "Josh, I think we need to send a QRF team down to the bridge, just in case some gang-bangers try to come across the bridge."

"I was thinking the same thing, Rich. I'll pick a QRF team and get them rolling. I'll go along with them."

"Uh, Josh, are you sure? I mean...."

"Yeah, Rich. There's not much of a likelihood for action, and three men could hold off a small gang that tried to cross where the bridge narrows down to one lane."

"OK. Take your walkie-talkie and keep me informed, OK?"

"WILCO, Rich."

Rich figured that the battalion had moved some of their forces into place the evening before, and hit the gangs from several different sides. Lieutenant Johansen had said that MS-13 controlled most of the city, and as the assistant intelligence officer, she should know. There were probably some other gangs that controlled smaller or more isolated areas.

He knew that MS-13 was the notorious and ruthlessly cruel Central American gang that was so prevalent in many American cities before the Collapse. He assumed that some of the Zulus had joined them also, or maybe they had carved out their own piece of turf where they used to hang out. He had no idea of how many MS-13 members there were, but they had to be pretty strong- after all only a few days after the Collapse they had run the Zulus out of town, and the Werewolves didn't even try to claim part of the city as their own. Regardless, the Army had to clear out all of the gangs in the city, since they had to establish security and control over the entire city so they could begin reconstruction.

In less than five hours, the fighting was all but over. There were occasional bursts of fire, probably when advancing squads came across some stubborn gang members. But the soldiers had protective vests and firepower that the gang-bangers didn't have.

Josh radioed back to Rich and said, "Rich we're coming back. Please open up the entranceway blockade for us. We saw most of the battle take place. It was quite a sight. I'll tell you more when we get back."

"Roger, Josh. See you then."

When Josh and the QRF team returned, Rich was already at the lake picnic area. He strolled down to Josh's house just as the QRF team was heading home.

"So, Josh, how did the attack go down?"

"Man, it was like being back in the sandbox again, watching a firefight from afar. We actually saw a pickup start over the bridge toward us once the Apaches went away but it looked like a Blackhawk C & C (command and control) helicopter saw them. They flew behind them and the door gunner took them out with just a few bursts. Letting any gang-bangers escape from the city in any direction was obviously not part of their game plan. Good thing, too. No sense in letting scum like that out to terrorize anyone else. But you know, even if the Blackhawk hadn't gotten them, we would have killed them all from the fighting positions we had dug on our side of the bridge."

"Well, let's hope that's all the shooting excitement we have for a long time."

Chapter 50

Rich had been wrong about something else. He had thought that the report from Colonel Marchione up to Brigade would eventually disappear on its way up the chain of command. In fact, it had made it all the way to the president last month, pretty much intact. The story was that compelling up and down the chain of command.

At the end of the staff meeting in Camp David, the last item, not on the agenda, was brought up by the SECDEF. "Sir, I want to read everyone a report we got yesterday. I want to do this because it's so unusual, and I think we all need to be aware of it. He then went on to read the report that had remained essentially unchanged that Lieutenant Johansen's boss, the battalion S-2, had given at the battalion command and staff meeting the morning after her meeting with Rich, Josh and the Gibsons.

After the SECDEF was through, the president looked around him and said to the others. "Damn, that is one hell of a story- simply amazing. I wonder how many other surviving groups like that there are? The president got a little emotional and said, "I want these people helped, Jim. And I want you and everyone else on this staff to look for more cases like this Sea Breezes community, and get them some help. He turned to the Chairman of the Joint Chiefs of Staff and said, "General, how long will it take to at least get these people some food?"

The Chief told them that the 1st Bn., 509th already had. A follow-up report mentioned that every soldier in the battalion had given up one of their daily MRE rations and that 600 MRE meals were delivered to the Sea Breezes survivors.

"Good. Good. Now, how long will it take to get them some more help?"

"Sir, the battalion doesn't have any food to distribute. Like everyone else, they are on survival rations of one or two meals a day. Right now, anything they give those civilians they have take from someone else.

"Also, we know that the battalion commander is planning a big operation against the gangs that control the city. Part of their mission is to seize control of the city and then call in some of the other agencies that can help set up a local government and repair the infrastructure. Port Monroe is one of the best options we have on the gulf coast- it has a good rail and road network to the interior, a deep-water port, and an oil refinery. Our experts say the refinery will be the toughest challenge to get operational, but that it can be done."

"I understand, General. But I want you to make this happen: After the battalion clears out the city and establishes security, I want you to put together a rescue team and send it down to the battalion. I want the team to take food and medical supplies, and go out there to that island and help those people. Get a camera crew and get the story from those survivors. I want TV and radio coverage of their story, and I want it put out on every news source we have in the U.S. By God, I want the story released to the international press also. I want everyone to see what a bunch of tough Americans can do when they're determined to fight and survive. Got that?"

"Yes sir," the General grinned. "Sir, in fact we've already put together a team just as you described. They're assembled in Ft. Benning, ready to go. All we have to do is give them the word. I, uh, anticipated your orders, Mr. President."

The president looked at him and just smiled. "Good man, Jim. OK, everyone that can, get out there and find the other Sea Breezes around the country. Let's start rescuing people that have hung on and held out. We need folks like them to get this country running again. There's not much sense in building back our infrastructure if there aren't any people left to use the facilities we build."

Chapter 51

Two days after the attack on downtown Port Monroe, Rich turned on the radio in the early afternoon to see if there was any interesting chatter. There was nothing for a few minutes and as he was about to turn the radio off to conserve the battery, he heard, "Colonel Cantrell this is the 509th. Over." There was a pause as Rich just sat there, looking at the handset as if it suddenly come alive, not believing he had just been called by name on the battalion's logistic radio net. The message was repeated and Rich snapped out of it, picked up the handset and answered, "This is Colonel Cantrell. What's up? Over."

There was a pause and it sounded like the radio operator dropped the microphone. After a scrambling noise, the operator came back, "Colonel Cantrell! We've been trying to get in contact with you for hours! Over."

"Roger. But I only monitor your net periodically since I don't have a spare battery. Over."

"Roger, sir. Stand by for the battalion commander. Wait, over."

Rich did, and in about a minute heard, "Colonel Cantrell, this is Colonel Marchione. How are you guys doing out there?"

"Not very well, Colonel. But we did enjoy the fireworks display you put on for us the other day. Was that door gunner that took out the truck heading our way from your command and control ship? Over."

Rich heard the Colonel laugh, "Yeah, that was us. No one was going to get away that easy. Fortunately the entire operation came off very well, just some final mopping up to do and the city will be clear of the gangs.

"Listen, the reason I'm calling is to let you know that as soon as you get off the radio, you should head out to the helipad. I've got another Blackhawk here loaded with 50 more cases of MRE's for you. And before you ask, no, my soldiers didn't have to give up one of their MRE meals to do this. The MRE's, and more, came all the way from the top. And I mean, from the very top.

"I'll tell you more when I get out there. I'll be coming in on my C & C ship after you've unloaded the MRE's. I'm also bringing our battalion doctor with me. I'd appreciate it if you could find him a place to stay overnight in case he has to. I'll see you at the helipad in about 30. Over."

Rich could hardly believe what he was hearing, but answered quickly, "Roger. I'll be there along with some of my neighbors. Over."

"Roger, Rich. Out."

Rich picked up his walkie-talkie and called Josh. When Josh finally answered he said, "Josh, they're bringing us another 50 cases of MRE's."

"Oh my God, Rich, that's great! When?"

"You won't believe it, but now, and I mean right now. I just talked to Colonel Marchione and he's coming too. Gather up some folks and three or four pickups and meet me at the helipad in 15 minutes."

"WILCO, Josh. This is great news! Wait 'til I tell Carmen!"

See you in a few, Josh. I'm going to go get Donna too, so she can be there."

"Good idea, Rich. See you soon."

By the time the first helicopter came into sight, Rich, Donna, and Josh, and about 15 other residents were standing off to the side of the helipad so they'd be well away from the Blackhawk's downdraft. Everyone was excited and talking at the same time. In a few minutes someone shouted and pointed up into the sky, "There it is! Over there. I see it."

The Blackhawk came straight in to the landing pad and set down easily. As soon as it set down, Rich and the others began offloading the MRE's onto the three pickup beds. When the last case was removed, the Blackhawk powered up from idle and took off. A few minutes later, Colonel Marchione's bird landed.

Colonel Marchione stepped out of the rear door, and Rich walked up to him with a big grin on his face. They exchanged a quick handshake, and Marchione patted Rich on the back. He turned around to his pilot and made a throat cutting sign for the pilot to shut down the engine. Colonel Marchione wanted to talk. Josh and Donna came up and joined Rich.

Once the blades had spun down and the noise lessened, Marchione repeated to the three of them the message he had gotten all the way down from the president. They all just stood there, amazed at the Colonel's words.

"Rich, that's it in a nut shell. Tomorrow you're going to be inundated by photographers, press and a medical team. Right now let me introduce you all to Major Phillip Coltrane." He turned to the man who had gotten off the Blackhawk after him and motioned him over and introduced him. They all shook hands and Marchione said, "Flip is my battalion doctor, and he's brought some medical supplies with him." Major Coltrane said, "Good to finally meet all of you. You and your neighbors have become quite famous over the past few weeks."

Rich smiled and said, "Welcome to Sea Breezes, Major." He turned back to Colonel Marchione and said, "Thanks, Bob, for everything you and your staff have done. Please convey to Lieutenant Johansen my thanks and our gratitude to all of your staff for having our back.

I'll let everyone know about the medical team at tomorrow's meeting. Meanwhile, I'll take Flip down to our aid station and introduce him to our doctor and nurse, and they can talk specifics about what we need in the way of medical supplies and assistance. We still have one woman in critical condition from a gunshot wound during the Zulu raid."

He looked back at Marchione and said "Bob, can you tell me when we can expect the medical team to arrive here tomorrow? I need to tell everyone tomorrow morning what to expect, and when."

"I think it'll be mid-morning, Rich. I heard maybe around 10 or so, but that may slip a little, depending on what else we have going on. Turn on your radio to the logistic net around 9:30 and we'll give you at least a 30 minutes heads up on their ETA. If you'll put out the word at your meeting, you can tell people in need of any kind of treatment to come to the aid station.

"Rich, I've got to take off and get back to my headquarters. My battalion still has lots of irons in the fire, but the one pertaining to your community is the most satisfying one we've had since we arrived here. Good luck, and since we'll need to be communicating with each other more often, keep your radio on all day during daylight hours."

Colonel Marchione pulled a radio battery out of his backpack and handed it to Rich. "Don't be afraid about running the battery down. You'll be getting a case of these tomorrow. We've hit the big time nationally, Rich. Let's make the best of it for everyone."

The two men shook hands, and Marchione jumped back into the Blackhawk and the blades spun up to take off.

Rich turned to Josh and said, "Josh, would you take the MRE's to Donna's house until tomorrow. I'm going to take Dr. Coltrane down to the aid station."

Josh said with a big grin still on his face, "Will do, Rich. I'll see you tomorrow at what's going to be the happiest morning meeting we've ever had."

Chapter 52

Rich took Major Coltrane to the aid station and introduced him to Dr. Rajan and Julia. They examined the wounded woman first, and Dr. Coltrane took a more powerful antibiotic from his medical kit and injected it directly into a vein in the woman's arm. He looked at the stitched up scars and complimented Dr. Rajan on his work. "We should see some improvement by tomorrow afternoon. Regardless, we'll Medevac her to our field hospital tomorrow so I can X-ray her and see if surgery is needed to repair any bone damage.

Dr. Rajan smiled and said, "Thank you, doctor." Dr. Coltrane then examined a couple of the other patients that were there for minor ailments and did what he could for them with medications Dr. Rajan and Julia didn't have available.

All of the residents spread the good news to their neighbors that evening and you could almost sense a giant sigh of relief. No one knew all the details yet, but they already knew they had more food, and now they also had something that was equally in short supply: Hope.

Rich went back home and told Sophia everything that had happened that day. They had a big meal and made sure Tasha got her fill. When they got through they didn't have much left in the house to eat, but they both understood that food would not be that big of a problem going forward.

Josh, Carmen, and Anita mirrored what the Cantrells had done, as had almost everyone else in the community. Everyone slept well that evening in Sea Breezes, except, of course, for the roof guards.

Chapter 53

The next morning, everyone who was able to showed up at the morning meeting. It was good to hear all the chatter and laughter again, something that had been very scarce over the past few months. Rich got up and began the meeting.

"Friends, we've been rescued!" That was followed by yells and cheers, and a lot of hugs, tears and back slapping.

Rich related the details of the previous day's events, including the details about the food and the coming visit later that morning of the photographers and a medical team. More cheers and back slapping.

"I want to say one thing before I turn this over to Dr. Coltrane. I've never been more proud of any group in my life than I am right now of all of you. We've endured the horrors of deprivation, danger, vicious attacks, and disease, and everyone here had the backbone to stand up to all of that adversity and endure. You are the best of what America is all about, and I'm looking forward to putting our guns away, and getting back to a normal life. It will take a long time- months if not years- before we worry about mowing our lawns and taking our kids to school again, but all of that is coming. We'll just have to work hard and do our part to help make it so."

There were raucous cheers when Rich quit speaking, and rather than try to introduce Dr. Coltrane, he just stepped down from the table as he gave a hand up for the Army doctor.

Dr. Coltrane waited until the crowd quieted down and looked out at all the happy, haggard faces. "Ladies and gentlemen, it's my privilege to meet such an outstanding group of men and women. I won't take a lot of your time, but I do need to tell you a few things.

"First, after this meeting we'll be delivering three MRE meals per person to every, man, woman, and child here. Second, as I'm told Dr. Rajan has warned you before, do not start eating full MRE meals now. Mix them up with your normal diet, and start off eating the more bland items, like applesauce, first. Your digestive systems just aren't ready for such a rich and spicy diet. I understand the gardeners are going to keep gardening and the fishermen are going to keep fishing. Use what they produce to slowly adapt yourselves to the new food.

"One last thing. This morning we'll have a full medical team fly in and they'll set up in a large tent in the front yard of the aid station. Anyone with ailments or in need of minor things like disinfectants, Band-Aids, anti-diarrheal tablets, or anything else, just show up after the team lands. I've also given some bottles of multivitamin and mineral tablets to Rich and they'll be handed out along with the MRE's. Take one a day- there's enough for 30 days for everyone.

It'll take the medical team an hour or two for them to set up, but when we're ready, we'll fire off a red star cluster flare so everyone will know we're open for business. Are there any questions?" If there were, everyone was too overwhelmed to ask them, so Dr. Coltrane stepped down.

Josh stood up and got everyone's attention. "Neighbors, we still have to keep our security up until the Army can clear the island." Good-natured boos and thumbs down followed, but Josh knew that everyone was just giving him a hard time. "Yeah, I know I'm the wet blanket at this party, but you know that all of the air activity here the past few days has attracted the attention of anyone and everyone left on the island. Let's not let our guard down now that we've come this far."

Most of the residents were nodding. After all these months they were still conditioned to self-preservation.

When Josh stepped down, Donna got up and had the last word before the meeting closed. "I just wanted to thank all of you for your support and confidence in me. I'll continue serving as your community arbiter but I doubt you'll need a judge and jury again, and by the time you do, I hope it'll be a proper legal system that administers the justice. I want to remind everyone that nothing will change overnight. We still have to dig our garbage pits, gather and purify our water, pull guard duty, work in the garden, send out our fishermen, and most importantly, keep helping each other out.

"I'll see you all around the community, but now let's get our three MRE's per person. Just remember what Dr. Coltrane said about taking it easy on the rich and spicy entrees. I still think it's a good idea to have morning meetings, so let's keep up that tradition for a while, if for no other reason than to socialize. I'll see you all here tomorrow at 9."

She stepped down and the meeting was over. People started cheering, a few "Way to go, Donna" were heard, and there was a lot of back slapping and kissing among couples that had put their personal life on the back burner for so many months.

Chapter 54

The rest of the day was a whirlwind of activity that left Rich, Donna, and Josh exhausted at the end of the day. The Army video crew had wanted all three community leaders to be present as they walked around Sea Breezes filming points of interest, such as the roof guard positions, the aid station, and the garden, so they could comment on everything. They even wanted to film the fishing "fleet" and the barricade at the entranceway.

They also asked for a demonstration of a QRF team rollout, but Donna put her foot down on that one. Her neighbors had a lot better things to do than become part of an action film. She made them settle for a description. But when they found out about Donna's QRF team's reaction during the Werewolves' attack, they insisted she give them a walkthrough of her part of the fight, from the rallying point to the end of the battle. She would end up being the fighter/heroine of the Sea Breezes documentary. As far as Rich was concerned, Donna was certainly the epitome of an armed citizen turned soldier in time of need, a sort of modern day "Minuteman;" or rather, "Minutewoman."

They spent a lot of time at the aid station, and made sure they got footage of the seriously wounded woman being Medevac'd back to the battalion's attached field hospital. Julia and Dr. Rajan got a lot of face time in the interview, and Dr. Rajan had to take them through the entire story of his captivity and experiences with the Werewolves.

Rich had to excuse himself when the battalion S-4, the Supply and Logistics Officer, flew in with a load of everything from more food to medical supplies, even toilet paper. When Rich saw the big plastic packages of toilet paper he thought, "That's probably going to be the second most appreciated item after the MRE's." and chuckled to himself.

The S-4, Major Sam Collins, explained that they would fly out once a month with enough MRE's for one per person every other day. That was all the nation could afford at this time for refugees and survivors who had some other sources of food. He also explained that they hoped to include things like canned goods and flour soon, once the nation's logistical system got up to speed. "That'll probably be a few months away, though." Rich thought that estimate was optimistic, but he didn't say so.

Major Collins added, "I'm glad to see you guys getting lots of attention, Colonel." Rich said he presumed they probably were, but that he wasn't going to turn anything down after all they had been through.

"We're all really glad to help your community get back on its feet. From what I hear, the Army and other federal agencies are directing a lot more of their resources to the search for, and rescue of, other surviving groups.

"Anyway, if you have any special requests for medical supplies or assistance you should use the radio you were given and ask for it on the battalion logistics net. As long as there is a real need, and we've got it and can supply without compromising our other missions, you'll get it." Rich thanked him and told him he wouldn't take advantage of the privilege, and only use the link in case of real need.

Anyone in Sea Breezes not directly involved in the tour and the resupply goings-on went about their daily business, albeit in a much better frame of mind. They knew that there would still be hardships for a long time, but they also knew that the worst was over. Knowing they wouldn't starve to death was a huge uplift to their spirits. They also knew that the extra food would allow them to work a little more each day, as well as keep some of the illnesses at bay.

The next morning, the Sea Breezes residents were again alone. Most people slept in, getting up only for breakfast in time to make the nine o'clock meeting, to see if anything new was going on. There wasn't, so the meeting was short, just a few reminders, and some questions about when electricity and other utilities would be restored, that no one had the answer to. Donna said she could only guestimate, and that it would probably be at least a year.

Rich and Sophia seated at their kitchen table, eating part of an MRE meal for lunch, when Rich got a call on the radio to let him know that Colonel Marchione needed to talk to him, and that he would fly into the helipad at 4 that afternoon. Rich said he'd be there with a vehicle.

When the helicopter touched down, Rich was at the helipad with his Outback. He picked the Colonel up and took him straight to his house. Sophia was waiting in the living room and when they walked in, Rich introduced the Colonel to her and to Tasha.

"It's good to meet you, Colonel."

"I'm pleased to meet you, Sophia. And please call me Bob" He looked down at Tasha, who sat by Sophia's side keeping an eye on the stranger at all times. So this is the famous Tasha, huh? The now nationally-famous super dog." Tasha looked up at him and just wagged her tail, once.

Sophia smiled and said, "Don't tell her that, Bob. It'll go to her head."

Bob chuckled and said "Rich, I wanted to talk to you about where we are on getting things up and running in Port Monroe. As you know, the president and his staff were very encouraged by your story. They were also pleased by the reports from the logistics and engineering experts that came here with us about getting the port and refinery operational again. Down the road, we're going to be putting together a civilian government- the whole shebang of mayor, city council, police, fire fighters, everything. We'll eventually restore water, electrical and sanitation services also.

"Of course that last part is a long ways off, but they're getting together some experienced men and women from all the services, refugee camps, and other federal agencies and sending them down here to start working on rebuilding the city's human infrastructure as well as the utilities. The fact is, Port Monroe, and Phelps Island, are going to be sort of guinea pigs to figure out how to recover and rebuild a city. They'll be copying everything that works here in as many other towns and cities as they can.

"So, here's what I'd like to know. Do you think there are people here in Sea Breezes that would be interested in helping fill out some of those positions?"

Rich thought for a moment and said. "Bob, I think it's safe to say that no one wants to do anything right now but keep the community safe and operating, and to look after their families and themselves. These people have been traumatized and they need some time to recover. Once you get the entire island and all of the city completely secured, they'll be ready to go to work doing something useful. I'll bring the subject up at tomorrow's meeting but don't expect any volunteers right now."

Sophia added, "I agree. I think in the back of everyone's mind they're asking themselves, 'What's next for me and my family?' I also believe they'll want to get back to work as soon as they can. No one expects to be given MRE's forever and just sit around here gardening and fishing."

Bob nodded and said, "Good. Please let everyone know that we're hiring, and that they don't have to decide tomorrow. You know these people, and they all had former careers and expertise in something. I'll leave it to you on how to approach the subject with them. In a few weeks I'll be able to put together a list of jobs we need filled and get it out to you.

"Starting next week my battalion is going to begin a concerted effort to find other survivors in and around the Port Monroe area, and get people to move into the city. There'll be plenty of homes that are vacant, and some teams from FEMA and other agencies are coming to try to find which homes in the area might still have survivors somewhere so we don't give those to the newcomers. You guys here in Sea Breezes have helped us a lot as far as security here on the island is concerned, and we think you can help us start getting the island repopulated, but it'll be a slow process.

"Tomorrow you'll be hearing some helicopters flying around the city and the island tomorrow with loudspeakers announcing that survivors should report to the bridge for food rations and medical care. They'll also be dropping leaflets with the same message.

"We're going to set up a couple of large tents on both sides of the bridge's entrances, with food and bottled water to hand out and an aid station to treat anyone sick or wounded. We know there are people out there and we have to bring them back into the fold of civilization. At this point, no one is going to be looking to prosecute anyone for minor crimes or transgressions they committed while trying to survive- short of outright murder, of course.

"When it comes time to allocate homes for them, we could use your help. You know a lot of homes here on the island where the owners are gone or dead. It's not the easiest process in the world to contemplate, but these are unusual times. If you or Rich could come around with the FEMA guys when they start inspecting houses, you could help by giving them any info you know regarding the occupants. Dr. Rajan can help us on that also when it comes to the houses in Sunset Beach. We don't want to give away houses to people just because they said they lived there before."

Rich replied, "Yes, several of us can help on that, and that's something we can do as soon as the FEMA teams are ready. We've gotten pretty familiar with everything on the island. You know, I suspect that once you get volunteers to help out in some of your projects, you might find some of them willing to go to work for you full time."

"Well, they won't be working for me. I'm just one slice of this cake. We've got government officials, construction workers, engineers, and a lot of other folks who'll start trickling in soon.

"The pay they'll initially receive will be just food and shelter, and maybe early access to some of the amenities of life as they become available. Everyone's been living in an essentially bartering and scavenging economy for the past seven months and it'll take a while to get the monetary system functioning again. You can expect gold and silver coins to be worth a lot soon, as a substitute for paper money. I heard that they're going to have to print and mint an entire new set of paper money and coins."

"All of that sounds very reasonable, Bob. And I'll put out the word at tomorrow's meeting so that everyone will know what's going on, especially so they won't be surprised when they hear loudspeakers blasting from helicopters. Is the anything else we can do to help out?"

"Not right now, Rich, but thanks. It's one step at a time for us too. By the way, speaking of some of the amenities of life, I have a personal gift for you." He went over to his backpack and pulled out two Cokes and a Mason jar filled with amber liquid and handed them to Sophia. "Sorry I don't have any ice cubes for you. You'll just have to rough it.

"Rich, I remember you from your days back at the Officers' Club in Ft. Bragg and noticed what you drank. We green Lieutenants looked up to you and your combat experience. I even started drinking Jack and Coke myself. That, by the way is not Government Issue. It's from my ever-dwindling personal stash. I doubt those Tennessee boys are going to be making any more whiskey for quite a while yet.

Rich laughed and said, "Bob, really, thank you. I'll make sure your gift is put to good use. I guess this is kind of a symbol we can look at as the beginning of working our way back to civilization as we knew it."

"You're welcome, Rich. Listen, I've got to head on back now. If you have any problems, call me on the logistics net. Sophia, it was good to meet you."

"Thank you, Bob. It's good to meet you too."

When Rich got back from dropping Colonel Marchione at the helipad, Sophia said, "Rich, why don't you call Donna, and Josh and Carmen on the walkie-talkie. Tell them to come on down to our house now. Tell them it's cocktail hour."

EPILOGUE

Two years later

It was almost eight o'clock Sunday morning. Sophia and Rich lay in their bed, still entwined after languishing in slow lovemaking until both were spent. Rich was looking at his sleepy wife, and thinking how much more beautiful she had become after her figure had filled back out since those terrible days in the months after the Collapse. She opened her eyes and caught him looking at her and said, "Whaaatt? Why are you staring at me?"

"Because I want to, and because I can. It's Sunday."

"Well don't get any ideas, Romeo, because you have to make some breakfast and I have to get started on next week's lesson plans. And, you need to cut the grass today."

"Yeah, OK. Hard to do, though, with just a lawn scythe."

"Oh, quit complaining. Go on now and fix us some breakfast. I'm going to take a shower."

"OK. Did you already plug in the coffee maker to make sure it works?'

"Yes, and it does heat up. Go down and put coffee in it and let's see if it'll make us a couple of cups of real coffee. It may not look like much esthetically, but Carmen bought one last week and she said it works just fine."

Rich lay there for a moment, thinking about the conversation they just had. He thought, "Quite a change from a couple of years ago."

They had bought the coffee maker the afternoon before at the Wal-Mart that had reopened just last month. They didn't have much of a selection, but new items were coming in almost every week, and the store was now open three days a week instead of two.

He walked into the kitchen, scooped out some coffee from a plain paper bag, and put it and some water in the pot and turned it on. It started percolating and the smell was wonderful.

Later that day they had to go to Donna's wedding. She was the police chief in Port Monroe now, and she had met a guy who worked in the mayor's office as the chief of staff. The two dated for seven months, had fallen in love, and decided to to get married. Good for her.

Rich and Sophia had met Donna's fiancée and they both liked him. He was ruggedly handsome and soft spoken, but he was a man of action and they fit together perfectly.

Josh and Carmen would be coming to the ceremony also, of course. Quite a few other couples from Sea Breezes had been invited too. The new couple would live in Donna's house in Sea Breezes.

It was a good thing they all had jobs now, so they could afford such luxuries as coffee makers and wedding ceremonies.

Donna and her new husband would spend their honeymoon at a hotel that had just opened the month before in Sunset Beach. The hotel was located in what had been one of the two condos there before.

The only thing remotely positive you could say about the Collapse was that unemployment was now almost zero. In fact, the entire culture of American society and work ethic had changed. If you didn't work and could, you didn't eat. Period. The partially disabled could do many useful things, such as filing papers and keeping records. They went to work every day also, proud of their contribution to the recovery. Even retired guys like Rich and Josh were expected to work, and pay taxes, until age 70. All government pensions in effect prior to the Collapse had been reduced by 50%, even though there weren't that many left to draw the monthly payments. Rich thought that that was OK. He enjoyed his new work.

He was still having difficulty getting used to the colorful and different sizes of the new dollar bills the government was issuing though. One thing he did appreciate was that the gold and silver coins he and Josh had saved were now worth almost three times as many new dollars as old ones.

Rich and Josh had opened a gun shop and firing range on the island. Carmen clerked and kept the books for the new business. They called it "Sea Breezes Firearms" and it was located in the same former coffee shop that the bridge guards had used, with a new open air firing range built behind it.

There was quite a bit of demand in the area now, since a lot of people who had never even held a pistol or rifle before the Collapse had gotten used to using them, and they wanted to stay in practice. A lot of newcomers to the area also wanted to learn to shoot, and who better to go to than the guys who had led the security of a nationally famous community of survivors?

The documentary on Sea Breezes the Army had made two years ago still played on TV from time to time, and that free advertisement certainly helped their business.

A lot of other Sea Breezes residents had found new jobs also. Martin Goldman went back to work in the Oil refinery. Fred Carlucci and Jacob Hanson were working in the port authority, running the docks. Karen Brown had remarried, to Martin Goldman, and was working in the Wal-Mart. Dr. Rajan and Julia had the Phelps Island Hospital running again. Julia just found out she was pregnant with Bill Norton's baby- they'd need to find a bigger home now that they would have three children, but they vowed to wait until one became available in Sea Breezes. No way were they going to leave this tightly woven community. Almost all of the other residents felt the same way.

Phase II behind Sea Breezes remained as empty of houses as ever. There were still a lot of homes and apartments that were unoccupied and available in and around Port Monroe and Phelps Island, so no one would be building any new houses anywhere on the island for a long time; or anywhere else in the country, for that matter. Construction workers were kept busy, however, with repairs and modifications, such as happened with Sea Breezes Firearms and the new hotel at Sunset Beach.

Rich grabbed three eggs from the refrigerator and made an omelet with mushrooms and onions that had come from "Sea Breezes Gardens".

Althea had become the proprietor of the growing business that had expanded through all of the Phase II area and beyond. Charlotte was her assistant manager, and the two still lived together in the same house. The eggs came from their poultry farm. No chickens were being slaughtered yet- they were too important to use as egg producers.

Rich opened up a can of pears to go along with the omelet. Unfortunately, there was no ham or bacon available yet. Fresh meats of all kinds were still scarce. None of the grocery stores had the facilities to process, store and refrigerate meat products yet. They hadn't even tried, since most of the meat being produced went into microwavables, MRE's, and canned goods that could be stored without refrigeration.

There were still a lot of areas in the United States that got no fresh produce whatsoever. Only MRE's and canned foods were available in most of the larger cities that were among those the government was trying to repopulate. And there were a lot of cities that the government had completely abandoned, at least for the time being. There just weren't enough people to warrant putting the entire infrastructure back together again in every town and city that had existed before the Collapse. The national government estimated that there were only about 100 million Americans that survived- less than one third of the pre-Collapse population.

Even the larger cities that were more or less functioning, and in various degrees, still weren't anywhere near the advanced state of some of the smaller towns that were easier to get back up and running. Port Monroe owed a lot to Sea Breezes for that, since they had a ready-made and skilled work force of almost 150 adults available right away.

It turned out that Sea Breezes wasn't as unique as people had thought. Once the government started looking, they found a lot of other communities that had survived the Collapse.

The vast majority were in rural areas, where they had the resources, knowledge and experience to make a go of it, living off the land. But there were even some entire small towns that had also survived.

There was a village in Mississippi, right on the river, that had survived pretty much intact. In fact many small towns that had access to bodies of water that they could fish managed to survive. There was another town up in the woodlands of upper Michigan that had made it also, by being in both hunting and fishing areas, and cooperating with each other. Several dozen other places that Rich had read about had also survived.

Sophia came into the kitchen in her bathrobe, still drying her hair with a towel.

"I smelled the coffee and couldn't wait. What's for breakfast?"

"Eggs and canned pears this morning, madam. Sorry we have no cream or sugar."

"Ha, like I care. I always drank it black anyway, even if you didn't."

After breakfast, Sophia cleaned up the dishes, and went into their converted office/bedroom to work on her lesson plans for her elementary students. She had a single class of children from 1st to 6th graders that she taught for eight hours a day, six days a week. Nowadays, the work week was six days for everyone, even kids going to school.

Rich put on his grubby shorts and shoes, and went out to cut the grass with his lawn scythe. He wanted to get it all done before he had to get ready for Donna's wedding.

While he was working, Greg and Rebecca Gibson walked by pushing a baby carriage with their 14 month-old son and waved at him. They had named him Leroy.

Everything just seemed so normal now.

If you enjoyed reading this book I would appreciate it if you would leave a review on Amazon. As a new author, ratings can make or break you. Just log onto the Amazon page for "Surviving in Sea Breezes," scroll down to "Customer Reviews," click on the block that says, "Write a customer review" and compose your comments. Thanks!

ABOUT THE AUTHOR

Douglas Thornblom is a retired Army Colonel and a graduate of the West Point class of 1966. After graduating from West Point, he earned his jump wings and his Ranger tab at Fort Benning, Georgia. During his 30-year Army career he served in combat in both Vietnam and El Salvador. He commanded an Airborne Infantry Rifle Company, a Mechanized Infantry Battalion, and a Basic Combat Training Battalion. He was also named a Senior Fellow at the State Department's Center for the Study of Foreign Affairs, and served three years as the Military Attaché to Spain.

He lives with his wife, Debbie, in Florida. They have a Siberian Husky named Sasha.

CPSIA information can be obtained
at www.ICGtesting.com
Printed in the USA
LVHW011607140922
728378LV00003B/406